One Plus One Equals Nineteen

One Plus One Equals Nineteen

Married: The Second Time Around

H. George Arsenault

Writers Club Press
San Jose New York Lincoln Shanghai

One Plus One Equals Nineteen
Married: The Second Time Around

All Rights Reserved © 2001 by Henry G. Arsenault

No part of this book may be reproduced or transmitted in any form or by any means, graphic, electronic, or mechanical, including photocopying, recording, taping, or by any information storage retrieval system, without the permission in writing from the publisher.

Writers Club Press
an imprint of iUniverse.com, Inc.

For information address:
iUniverse.com, Inc.
5220 S 16th, Ste. 200
Lincoln, NE 68512
www.iuniverse.com

ISBN: 0-595-17162-1

Printed in the United States of America

Dedication

This book is dedicated to Delores, my loving wife of thirty three years, and to our seventeen children, who made our *joint venture* such a happy and wonderful journey by giving us all their unselfish love and devotional support through out the years.

Preface

What's in a Title? *What rationale would persuade a single man with seven children and a single woman with ten children to marry and have a family of nineteen?*

To examine this query, I originally planned this work to be in two phases, that is, two books. Book one would be the story of my original family with seven children, and book two would be the story of the added eleven dependents. The title would be *Seven Come Eleven*. I planned book one to shed some light on my early environmental background…my single years and my first marriage experiences that had conditioned me to take on this new responsibility with any hope for success. It would narrate a lot of my thinking up to the time I was left with my seven small children after my wife died. Book two would relate the many problems and their solutions that we encountered with a family of nineteen and our many attempts to teach the children the difference between right and wrong, and our "preachings" for their edification and guidance. We felt they would have a better chance in life if we did our job well. After friends critiqued my first drafts, they said it was like a song with highs and lows melting in with the symphony of life. They encouraged me to publish this manuscript. Later, when rewriting my manuscript, I was fortunate to obtain some astute counseling from a former Holy Redeemer School acquaintance, the renowned mystery writer William X. Kienzle, who had written at that time more than twenty mystery novels, including the *Rosary Murders* which was made into a movie of the same name. Bill's wife,

Javan, a retired proofreader and editor from the Detroit Free Press, reviewed my manuscript and made many corrections. After talking with Bill and Javan, I again changed the title to simply *Seventeen* and book's one and two were combined into one manuscript. Having been rejected by several publishers and at Bill Kienzle's suggestion, I solicited Berl Falbaum, an author and professional public-relations specialist, former reporter for The Detroit News, and teacher at two state universities, to assist me in the final rewrite version of my manuscript for self- publication. I then continued my effort to combine the two parts into one book and returned to the title *Seven Come Eleven*. But after many discussions with Berl and his suggestion that I focus on "seventeen," it became clear to me that because of the total distinction and uniqueness of the two parts, I really had two stories that could not be told together as one book. The "book one" part is much like a Shakespearean tragedy that tells the story of how fate, with the *slings and arrows of outrageous fortune,* had dealt an average man a devastating blow destroying his "blue heaven." "Book two" is a light-hearted comedy that tells the story of how one widow and one widower merged in a joint venture of marriage to raise seventeen children. "Book one," the tragedy, was abandoned for now. And, at the suggestion of Berl, my astute critic and proofreader, the final result and title of my "book two" is now called *One Plus One Equals Nineteen*. Thus, I hope *One Plus One Equals Nineteen* answers for readers the question why Delores and I formed a union to raise seventeen children. More important, we hope readers will learn of the immense joy and love we have experienced through out the years.

Acknowledgements

Delores A. Arsenault: Graduate of Marygrove College, teacher, mother, and my dear wife and constant companion. Thank you for your love, wit, wisdom, and your unfailing support for thirty-four years. You have been my faithful partner giving me strength and guidance during all these many years. *You're right from heaven...oh, I know your worth. You've made a heaven...for me...right here...on earth.*

Seventeen Arsenault/McMillan Children: You know who you are. Thank you for being the best, the brightest, and the kindest, most considerate children in the world and making your mother and me the proudest parents in the world.

The Dominican Sisters: We are especially indebted to the Dominican Sisters who taught our large family when we were just starting our marriage. In the first year of our marriage, they accepted six young Arsenaults at St. Clare of Montefalco School, making a total start of ten Arsenault/McMillan's in their school. Their total enthusiastic encouragement, prayers, and kind consideration, will always be part of our gratitude.

Friends and Relations: A special thanks goes to all our friends and relations who have been our encouragement and faithful supporters in this challenging experience from the very beginning. It was with their good wishes and prayers that helped us succeed.

I

Strangers

---

*Every heart has its secret sorrows, which the world knows not,
And oftentimes we call a man cold when he is only sad.*
Longfellow 1807-1882

My wife, Marge, died of a brain tumor in May 1964, and I found myself a single man with seven children, trying to avoid the reality of my sorrows. I became cold in my empathy for others. I lost the joy of living each day. I just wanted to get away…go away. I was a stranger in a world where life had no future for me. I knew that I was grieving and I had concern for the children's loss as well and so, a few weeks later, I decided to take the six oldest children on a two-week vacation to visit my uncles, aunts, and cousins in Quebec, Canada. My two-year-old baby, Janet, stayed with my widowed mother, who had taken care of her the past year while Marge was in and out of the hospital. Taking this vacation to Gaspe', Canada helped take my mind off myself, but when we returned from this vacation, I was still miserable.

How can you have a house full of kids and still be alone? Analogy: lost in the middle of the ocean on a raft…water, water everywhere and not a drop to drink. A single parent having a large family is not the best situation. Now, without my wife, I had to make all the family decisions alone.

As I adjusted to this new single-parent life, Saturday night became my night to go out and find distractions. As my brother said, "Do something...visit somebody." So, on Fridays, after work, I would pick up my mother and baby Janet and bring them to my house in Allen Park. She would stay every weekend with the children. On Sunday, after church, I would return my mother and Janet to my mother's house. During the week, I had numerous housekeepers, nannies, and baby-sitters. But, on the weekends, my mother provided a means for me to seek some diversions and distractions in my sorrow.

But visiting old friends, alone, didn't work out too well. I could tell that they were uncomfortable and so was I. What do you talk about? My problems were not theirs. We had nothing in common anymore. My loneliness seemed to thunder out at me in my mind as I struggled to find a subject to talk about. Finding and making new friends is easier said than done.

I went to the Thunderbowl Lanes bowling alley near my home in Allen Park and I was told that a mixed league on Sunday afternoon needed bowlers. So, I signed up to bowl with a group of single people who were in there twenties. They were about ten years younger than me. However, this diversion helped to wile away the time...take my mind off my problems. The bowlers were all very nice...but I still felt somewhat out of place.

During the following summer...in 1965, my brother, Al, tried to help me by suggesting that I join some clubs, and meet new people. I didn't feel much like doing either. I was still melancholy and filled with self-pity. But Al persisted. He had read in the local papers about a group at the YMCA called *Parents Without Partners*, and another group, that he had read about in the Michigan Catholic newspaper called *The Naim Conference* which consists of only Catholic widows and widowers. "And it's not all old people," he said "I read that they have an age limit of fifty-five. These clubs are for guys like you. They have dances and other diversions like picnics for the children. You might enjoy their activities."

"Thanks, but I'm not in the mood."

"You should give it a try," he persisted, ignoring my protests. "Go to one of their meetings."

"Okay, okay," I relented. " I'll give it a try. But don't worry about me so much. I'll get by."

Parents Without Partners

The first meeting I attended was that of Parents Without Partners in nearby Lincoln Park because of the proximity to my home. Almost all the women and men I met were divorced. I also discovered that the ratio between the women and men was about six women to every man. Most were about my age and with children. They all were congenial and polite and I felt comfortable talking to them, because we all had similar problems raising children without spouses. During the next few months, I met many single parents who said to me, "It's good to get away and talk with adults for a change." Also, when the children are small, there is a need to evaluate issues, problems, and decisions with an adult. Independent decision-making is not the most desirable method. Joint or group decision-making increases the number of decisions that are correct.

I felt sorry for the divorced mothers because they really had it tougher financially. They had to raise the kids with little support from the fathers. They had to provide for themselves, so that most had to find work, usually starting at the bottom of the wage ladder. Many had little or no credit and drove old cars that always needed repairs, while their former husbands were living like bachelors, working their usual jobs without worrying about the kids. Free as birds, they could run around to bars, go fishing or hunting on weekends, or whatever, without a worry in the world and many times they were late with their child-support payments.

Naim Conference

The night I went downtown to attend my first Naim Conference meeting, I again realized that I was not the only one who had lost a partner to death. A widower named Pat Lynch met me at the door. He introduced himself and I gave him my name. He asked me what parish I was from and how long I was a widower.

The usual inquiry, I thought. "I'm a member of St. Mary Magdalen parish and I live in Allen Park. I've been a widower for over a year."

He asked me how many children I had, and I told him seven.

"I want you to meet a widow that has ten children, and she's about your age."

"Ten! Where does she keep them all?"

He introduced me to Delores. Delores said she lived on the *east side* of Detroit in Grosse Pointe Park. I told her I was from the *west side*. She told me that she had lost her husband of fourteen years to a sudden heart attack three years earlier…in 1962. She said she had heard a thud noise upstairs, as if something heavy had fallen. When she went upstairs, she found him lying on the floor. She called for help but it was too late. He had died of a sudden, unexpected, massive heart attack. She said that she was three months pregnant with her tenth child, and her oldest, Donald, was in the eight grade. Talk about *the going getting tough*…I reflected again that I wasn't the only one that fate had given a bad deal.

Everyone in the Naim group had their own sad story, since they were all widows and widowers. I was introduced to many people, and one young widow, Helen Johnson, lived just a few blocks from me in Allen Park. She too was another widow who had lost her husband to a heart attack, although he had been under a doctor's care for many months before he died. She had a couple of daughters who went to school with some of my children. She said she met my son Patrick while she was a part-time teacher at St. Mary Magdalen grade school. She said that many times Pat looked like he was not paying attention, but when she would question him, he always had all the right answers.

Delores was the activities chairperson. She announced that there was a dance coming next Saturday evening. "Don't miss the Saturday night dance!" she said to all, when giving her report. Helen Johnson came over to me and asked if I was going to the Saturday night dance. I said I would like that and because we lived near each other, why don't I pick her up and save one car. She agreed and I said I would pick her up at seven o'clock sharp.

Dinner Dance

The night of the dinner dance was a balmy summer evening and a good-size crowd was there. The music was great and everyone that could dance was dancing. Helen, whom I had driven to the dance, was dancing with someone and, not being much of a dancer, I was sitting at a table watching. Suddenly, from across the room, I saw an arm waving at me. It was Delores. She was waving at me to come and dance. I went to the dance floor where this "five foot-two, eyes of blue" met me. What a dancer. I had taken five lessons from Arthur Murray's when I got out of the army and knew only the basic magic-box-step. I never was a good dancer! Delores, however, was a beautiful dancer. She reminded me of the dance instructors at Arthur Murray's, who made dancing look so easy. We were doing so well that when the music stopped, we kept right on dancing. I could hear Frank Sinatra singing, "*The band had left the stand and we were still dancing, somewhere on a cloud, off in the blue.*"

I had started the evening with Helen but this sensational brunette, named Delores, had taken my breath away. A year later Sinatra would be singing his hit song, Strangers *in the Night,* and with Barbara Streisand's hit, *People.* These two songs seemed to say the things that explained this encounter in this enchanted night.

As the party was breaking up and the dancing was over, I asked Delores, "What's your phone number? Maybe I could give you a call some night when all the children are in bed and we could go out for coffee."

She gave me her phone number and that's how *it* all started…just a couple of people who enjoyed each other's company. It isn't an easy job for any parent who is a widow or a widower without a partner to be the mother and the father to a lot of children. It's hard on the parent and on the children. I know because I was struggling to keep my family together much as my widowed mother had done for my sister, my brother, and me thirty years ago. The compatibility with people in the same circumstances getting together helps each of them do a better job as parents when they have some adult with the same problems to talk to. That's what the Naim Conference club was all about. It was a supportive club group where I met new friends…friends that were congruous and empathic to my situation. It turned out that my brother was right.

II

People

I love these little people; and it is not a slight thing, when they, who are so fresh from God, love us.
—Charles Dickens—1812-1870

Joining the Naim Conference was a turning point in my life. I met so many nice people who were in my same situation. We were people who needed people. Everyone had a family to worry about and everyone appreciated the mutual esteem and friendship that the club provided. In just a couple of meetings, I had met someone who made me forget my troubles. I just couldn't get her out of my mind.

A few nights after the dance, I called Delores and asked her if she would like to go out for coffee. She said she would and gave me the directions to her house, and I was off for my first of many trips to Delores's home in Grosse Pointe Park.

I noted the coincidence that I lived in Allen Park on Hanfor Street and Delores lived in Grosse Pointe Park on Balfour Street. We both lived in *parks* and both of our street names ended with *four*. Hanfor and Balfour. Interesting!

When I arrived, I found Delores's house to be a large colonial brick home. Makes sense, I thought, her with ten children. Delores answered the door and stated that it didn't take me long to get there. I told her that it was only seventeen minutes of freeway driving.

"You have a nice size house for your large family," I observed as she led me into the front living room.

"It's adequate. One needs a large house for a large family. Isn't that right?"

"Right! It doesn't make sense to bring children into poverty. Does it?"

"Why do you say that?"

"Well, having a family with ten children takes a lot of resources. One needs to have the means to properly house and nurture a large family so they can get a proper start in this crazy world. Don't you agree?"

"Really?"

"Yes, really. Tell me, why is it so quiet around here? Where are all your children?"

"Oh, they're around. Some are downstairs in the game room, and the others are in the den watching television."

"Are they all as nice as you?"

"They're nicer. You'll see when you meet them. I'll call them when you're ready. They're all anxious to meet you."

"I'm ready."

I sat down on the couch while Delores called the children. Suddenly, in they came from what seemed like all directions.

"This is Mr. Arsenault," she said as they entered the room.

They were all very polite and they impressed me as admirable children, much like my own. I couldn't help making some comparisons between her children and mine as she introduced them to me.

"Are these all of them?" I asked.

"No, my two older boys, Doc, sixteen, and Bob, fifteen, are away studying at the Augustinian Seminary in Holland, Michigan."

"Must be smart boys."

"All my children are smart."

"But why do you call your oldest 'Doc'? Does he plan to become a doctor?"

"No, his name is Donald Robert and his father used his initials DR and nicknamed him Doc. The second oldest is named Robert James."

"Sounds like some kind of a tradition starting, Donald Robert, Robert James, the third boy must be named James-something."

"Could have been. But my third-born was named Timothy John. He should have been named James Timothy or James John, but tradition was thrown out and here is fun-loving Timothy John in person."

"Hello, Mr. Arsenault," he said as we shook hands.

"Then came Joseph Patrick," Delores said.

"There's a coincidence. I have a Patrick Joseph."

Joe stepped forward and, shaking my hand, he said, "I'm Joseph McMillan." Then he offered me his hand again. Shaking his hand a second time really made me feel welcome.

"Joe is our Mr. Fix-it around here," Delores said. "Whenever we have anything broken, we just put it on his workbench and Joe fixes it."

"Every family needs a Mr. Fix-it."

After Joe, I met Martin Dennis and Steven Thomas.

"How old are these two handsome boys?"

"Marty is eight and Steve is six years old."

"My two youngest boys are Robert Ernest and Mark Anthony. They're seven and six "

Delores next introduced me to her four girls. "Another coincidence," I said. "I have four girls too."

"This is my youngest," Delores said, "Mary Ann McMillan."

"Just as pretty as your mother. And how old are you, Mary Ann?"

"I'm two," she said with a cute little smile.

"My youngest is Janet Frances and she's also two years old."

Then I met "sweet Sue"…Susan Jane McMillan…her five-year-old, who was the same age as my *sweet* Aileen. I then met Ann Louise, a nine-year-old. "And when were you born?" I asked her.

"I was born on October 16, 1955."

"You were born a year and two months to the day of my daughter Margaret Elizabeth," I said. "She is seven years old but you both were born on the sixteenth of the month."

Then I met Delores's oldest daughter, Patricia Marie. "We call her 'Tish' for short," Delores said. "Tish is eleven years old."

"Tish is the same age as my daughter Mary Ann," I said. " I bet she's as big a help to her mother as my Mary Ann is to me."

"She sure is," Delores said. "But all my children are a big help."

The house was as neat as a pin and so were the children. What an organizer this Delores is, I thought. What a homemaker and manager she must be, to be able to run this large family all by herself, and still have time for the to be Activity Chairperson for the Naim Conference take some doing.

"I'm impressed," I said. "It seems like you have everything under control."

"What do you mean 'control'?"

"I mean that you're a very capable mother."

"Well, when necessity calls, one learns fast," Delores said.

"Yes, you're right, necessity is the mother of invention," I said, quoting an axiom.

"No you don't. You're not pinning that on me," Delores said.

"Oh, you're not the mother of an inventor," I said as we both laughed.

Good sense of humor and pretty too, I thought.

We drove to Kapitski's, a restaurant on Mack Avenue, just two blocks from Delores's home. We talked about the weather and how pleasant it was to get out for a nice breath of fresh air and some conversation after a busy day. Delores said that it was fun to be able to chitchat with an adult after a full day of ten children and all that goes with it.

"Here you are," the waitress said, as she placed two cups of coffee before us.

"Thank you, Ann," Delores said, reading the nametag on the waitress.

"Do I know you two?" the waitress asked.

"No. This is our first time here," Delores said. "If you knew us you wouldn't forget us."

"Why is that?"

"Well," Delores said, "you see, I'm a widow and he's a widower and together we have seventeen children and we're engaged to be married."

"I can't believe it," the waitress said. "Hey, Mable," she said turning to another waitress nearby clearing a table. "Do you know how many children this young couple have?"

"No, how many?"

"Seventeen! This nice young couple has seventeen children together and they are engaged to be married. Can you believe that?"

Everyone in the place was now looking at us.

"Well, bless my soul," Mable said. "God bless them."

I couldn't believe my ears. What was Delores saying? This was our first time out and she's telling the waitress we're engaged to be married and that we have seventeen children. "Delores," I said in a whisper, "what are you telling these people?"

"Oh, I just wanted to see the look on their faces."

"Look on their faces? Delores, you surprise me. I never expected a refined person like you to tell the world about the number of children you or we have and then stated that we are engaged to be married. Are you kidding?"

"Of course I'm kidding. What do you mean 'number of children we have'?"

"I mean I never tell people that I'm a widower with seven children, all under twelve years old. It leads to too many questions and I feel that I have to defend my situation. They wouldn't understand."

"Oh, I don't know," she said. "I always tell everyone I know that I have ten beautiful children. I even carry pictures in my purse to show them."

Removing a large wallet from her purse, Delores unfolded a whole string of pictures of her children.

Well, I learned something about Delores. She was a woman with a real sense of humor and she was happy and proud of her family. I realized she had a point.

"OK, you're right to be pleased with your family," I said. "But did you have to tell them we were engaged to be married? Really, Delores, you've got the whole restaurant talking about us. Look over there at that table near the door. The waitress is telling them and they're looking right at us. Let's get out of here. They'll be talking about us after we leave."

"Oh, you're just imagining things."

"Delores, let's get out of here before you tell another story."

"George, don't be so serious. It's just for fun."

"Sure, just for fun," I said as I got up and put some money on the table for the bill.

Diamond Ring

A couple days later, we went to another restaurant, a pizza place on Jefferson, not too far from Balfour Road. This time I was prepared for Delores' "announcement" of our engagement. I had gone to a novelty store and bought a big glass "diamond" engagement ring for ten dollars. I went to a jewelry store and bought a beautiful box for the ring for a couple more dollars. As we were sipping our cup of coffee and talking about children, I took out this little box from my pocket and said, "Here's a little something for you." I handed her the little package wrapped with a gold ribbon.

"Oh, George," she said, as she carefully opened the package and revealed the large "diamond" ring with a little note inside the box.

WILL YOU MARRY ME?
Love,
C'est moi
George

"Oh, George…you shouldn't have…and look at the size of this diamond…It's so big. George…no, no…I really couldn't. You really shouldn't have done this. It's too soon, too fast. I need time to think. No, take the ring back and get your money…I can't accept this. I need more time," she said as she handed the box back to me.

"You just take all the time you want," I said refusing to accept it. "You keep the ring no matter what your decision is. It'll be just a token present of our friendship."

"I've never seen one that was self-adjustable before," she said as she took it out of the box and saw the split band. "This must be something new," she said as she began to realize the true value of the ring. "It seems like a good idea, doesn't it?"

"Yes," I said. "That's the way it is when you buy the very best. You get the latest fashion and design."

"You devil!"

"Now we're even," I said. "After that little engagement party you pulled on me the other night, I thought that you deserved some special gift."

"But…that was just for fun."

"This is just for fun too."

We were just dreaming out loud. At the time, we both knew marriage was a serious commitment not to be taken lightly…but wouldn't it be nice if it were possible?

The conversation turned to the feasibility of two people like us forming a partnership in marriage and raising seventeen children. "What would people say if we told them we were really thinking of getting married and raising seventeen children in one household?" I said. "I shudder to think about it."

"But what can they say? They would probably try to talk us out of it."

"Can you believe that if two people like us were to ever marry…the problems there would be? Think of it, seventeen children and a wife would make me the unique wage earner with nineteen dependents. Wow! The computers at General Motors would close down. Uncle Sam's IRS would never believe us."

"Well, I guess that any taxpayer who suddenly increases his dependents from seven children to seventeen children does seem a little unusual," Delores said.

"No big deal," I said. "Doesn't it happen every day?" We both laughed.

III

Who's Who

The family was ordained by God . . . the first form of the church on earth. William Aikman
1682-1731

When one suddenly meets ten new people, whether they are adults or children, it's not easy to remember their names. Everyone wants to be called by his or her name and that goes for children too. When I first met Delores's children, I thought that nametags would have been a big help to me. But, it became easier to remember who's who after many months getting to know them. However, remembering their birthdays required more effort. I knew that we had a birthday in every month of the year except August. Some months had two birthdays,…February, April, May, June, and July. We even had one month with four birthdays. March and two of those were on the tenth of March. Seemed easy enough. As to whose birthday was on a given day, we needed to look at the program listing.

Joint Venture

As we met more and more often, we kept talking about our two families, noting the similarities and coincidences, and there were many. During the autumn months that followed, we talked about the future. We seemed to find ourselves very much in love, and marriage was a subject that we had discussed but seemed out of the question. A family of nineteen would demand a lot from everybody. But as time went on and weeks turned to months, a possible marriage, or, as I called it, a merger and joint venture, became a subject we discussed often and more seriously.

Meanwhile, I found that each day was another happy day to talk to Delores. She was great and fun to be with. Her sparkling personality and good humor along with her good common sense captivated me. As the song said, *I'm just like putty in the hands of a girl like you*. I was crazy about *the kisses of Delores*.

I wrote Delores a letter telling her how much I loved her. Delores liked my letter and told me to keep writing. So I spent many a night writing Delores, telling her how much she meant to me and telling her how she had turned my life around and let me *walk in the sun once more*. Delores would write me notes and sign them *ME*. Now here was another coincidence. My wife, Margaret Elizabeth, left me notes signed *ME*. So, I when I left her notes, I signed my name as *ME* but in French: *c'est moi*, meaning *it's* me, or it's I.

We went to see many stage shows in the area. The songs in *Camelot; C'est Moi* and *If Ever I Would Leave You*, fitted right in with our romance. We saw *My Fair Lady* and *I've Grown Accustomed to Her Face* and *I Could Have Danced All Night* seemed to have been written just for us.

Everything seemed to point to our love for each other and the eventuality of our marriage and the merging of our two families into a seemingly impossible joint venture began to become more and more plausible.

"Delores, I have a present for you. It's a copy of *Who Gets the Drumstick* by Helen Beardsley. It's the story of a family of eighteen children with a widow and widower as the father and mother. This is the book that the movie *Yours, Mine and Ours* were based on. I thought that it's too much a coincidence to ignore."

"Yes, I read about that movie with Lucille Ball and Henry Fonda. We'll have to see it. I hear that after they were married, they had two more children, thus it was *your* children, *my* children, and *our* children. However, for us it will be only *our* children even if we have another, they will all be *our* children. Agreed?"

"Of course, I agree. It's the writing on the wall, Delores. Heaven is sure trying to tell us something. If we don't get married and make a go of this thing, we're apt to be struck down by a bolt of lightning."

"Well, if it can be done, it'll take a lot of planning and a lot of praying," Delores prudently said.

"The children all seem to get along fine," I submitted. "And, Financially you have as much income as I have, so together we can cut our overhead of maintaining two houses and have only one large house. That should be a big cost savings. General Motors will pay the medical insurance of all of us. There's several hundred dollars of savings per month right there. I'm sure we can do it financially. You've heard of that movie *Cheaper by the Dozen*. Ours will be cheaper by the dozen and a half."

"Maybe if we say a *Novena* together, everything will work out," Delores suggested.

"Sure, I'll say a novena with you. What are the prayers and for how long?"

"It's a Novena booklet with special prayers to our blessed mother and you have to say it every day for twenty seven days of petitions and twenty-seven days of thanksgiving. Will you do it?"

"Why not. I remember reading of some saint that said, *pray as if everything depended on God and work as if everything depended on you.* If that's the key to success, how can I argue?"

"A marriage like ours will not be easy and we know of a few marriages where a widow and widower combining two families of children that ended up in the divorce courts."

"Yes, I know. And they were small families of five and seven. One couple where the wife had one fifteen-year-old boy and the husband had five of his own went on to have another baby together for an *ours,* and they failed."

"But, there was a big flaw," Delores said. "That husband became an alcoholic and that's why they failed."

"Well, we don't have the time nor the money to become alcoholics," I said.

"One Naim Conference widow who married had a nervous breakdown. And remember the mother who had one teenage boy married the widower with five small children? The small children just could not accept the new mother."

"You're right. Some of these marriages should never have happened. It's not easy for sure. The children's agreeing to the union is very important."

"I think all our children appear to be happy together. But, we'll say the Novena anyway, and maybe Heaven will help us. I said a Novena before my first marriage and it turned out all right," Delores said.

"It's all right by me and it can't hurt anything. I'm willing to say the Novena if you are. Just saying these prayers in this small book for fifty four days should do it, right?"

"That's right," Delores explained, "twenty seven days petition and twenty seven days thanksgiving whether you think you got the favor or not. That's the Novena and it only takes about fifteen minutes each day."

"It doesn't make much sense to pray 27 days thanksgiving if you don't get the favor."

"The premise is that you really did get an answer and the answer was '*no!*' That means that it was better for you not to get the favor."

"Meanwhile we'll continue planning," I said. "I'll make up a budget, and we'll start looking for a home big enough for seventeen children. We can't get married until we find one…that's all there is to that.

We'll just say it's God's will," Delores added, "and we'll keep going the way we are now with separate families. One can raise a family in a small house but one cannot start with a big family unless one has a suitable house for them. Don't you agree?"

"Yes! Unless everything works out, the marriage will have to wait. However, when we do find the right house, we can start our *joint venture*. We're like two companies who join forces to achieve an objective. I'll put it in writing and send you *An Analysis of Unity* hypothesis for this joint ventured in my next letter."

The following is my *Analysis of Unity* hypothesis that I wrote and sent to Delores with the hope of convincing her that this marriage was both economically feasible as well as socially acceptable. I tried to plan this union, as a businessman would devise a business plan.

Analysis of Unity

What benefits can we expect by uniting these two separate *companies* into a single joint venture operating as one entity? Along with the happiness of nineteen people, we could cite the economics of scale cost savings. The saving benefits of thrifty buying in larger quantities along with the savings realized from other joint planning will be our goal.

For example, since our separate families were subsisting and managing as separate and independent families, we could expect financial savings right from the start by combining resources and efforts. By using one home for both families, we could expect to immediately save on utilities, property taxes and home insurance. The cost of GM's MIC General auto insurance provided approximately a twenty percent discount on the cost of collision, comprehensive coverage, property damage, bodily injury, personal injury insurance costs when a second car was part of the insurance package. This was a substantial savings for auto insurance. We could expect to reduce our overhead costs for taxes, gas, electric, water and telephones costs between Allen Park and Grosse Pointe Park and show considerable savings. By careful planning, we could expect to reduce the cost of many other items, using large-scale purchasing power and discounts.

By careful planning and organizing, we can also expect to create efficiency in the duties and chores required for a first class family. The proper use of the available manpower (nine boys and eight girls) would lighten the tasks around the house and with fewer burdens for everyone and produce the best good housekeeping standards with a minimum of effort by everyone. The increased efficiency along with the interchange of vital data of past experiences between and with the added advantage of many heads *brain storming* for the common goal, should produce a decided reduction of the load and burden on top management (you and I) thus providing an increase of the happiness and joy for all the members of this new joint company (family).

The development of this thesis as we continue should result in more benefits for this joint venture. With careful examination and testing, these savings and efficiencies could be expected to continue as new ideas and methods are developed from time to time, contributing to the ease and comfort of all members of the company. It was more than probable that every one of us could increase our efficiency more than fifty percent, thus increasing our happiness and joy more than one hundred percent.

The primary and most valuable reason of uniting our mutual love is for the total consideration of others. The love of two individuals that emphasizes the unselfish consideration for others (the children) is a powerful force, which can bring the joy of great accomplishment within our reach as well as provide the children in the family the happiness of growing up with loving parents and brothers and sisters. Our objective will be to raise our girls to be perfect ladies and our boys to be perfect gentlemen.

The communication with those we love and the example of our love can provide the essential ingredients for individual personal happiness as well as the salvation of their very souls. We must face the facts and not fail to realize the benefits of this association for the good of all. If I were God, and I had two people,…a man and a woman…who were willing to be the father and mother to seventeen very valuable children, I would make it easy for them to make this happen. The fears, worries, and anxieties that may stem from this proposal can be dealt with adequately and successfully with the proper planning, organizing and control by the managers.

Love can produce poise, satisfaction, self-confidence and bountiful energy in all members of the family. With our trust in God and His unselfish love, we could create a beautiful symphony for God. These seventeen children may someday be the elements that can contribute to the greatness of God in the world. This was not a matter of chance but a positive trust in God that would help us to succeed in our venture.

Look at the fun we would have proving that unselfish love can conquer all obstacles making this joint venture a success. If we could manage to be wise enough to learn the right things and avoid learning the wrong things, then success would be guaranteed. It would be a challenge devoutly to be desired. The greatest treasure of life which cannot be corrupted and which we can take with us into the next world is pure love…true unselfish love…a divine reflection of God Himself. And remember, with God, all things are possible.

Step Parents

So, a joint venture of marriage and the combining of our families of seventeen children were agreed upon providing we felt we could solve the problems that would come with this alliance. Will this marriage last? Can two people raise seventeen children and do a good job? Can the different personalities in children cause incompatibility? Will the children accept the stepparent? How do you raise seventeen children and have them grow up as good loving people who are honest, kind, considerate, ambitious and hard working citizens of this great country? These were some of the questions that people asked when we first talked about the impending marriage. I think that it all depends on what the similarities and the differences are in the parents. Some differences are good since *opposites attract* and *variety is the spice of life*. But unity and unity of purpose, and setting good examples by the parents, is the common bond. Respect for each individual child as a unique gift from God was also part of our common bond.

"Can it succeed?" We were not sure when we first started. It took the solving of each problem on a day-to-day basis in order to make a venture like this work. Everyone in the family knew that this was necessary. They all knew that everyone would have to help to make it a success. But they knew that it was a worthwhile venture that would reap tons of rewards. They knew that they could be better than they were.

Delores and I knew that it would not be an easy task. There were many problems, the most immediate being the sale of both our homes and finding one big enough to accommodate the new family. How much money would we need and how large a mortgage could we afford to take on? The house would have to have six or more bedrooms with baths and that's a big house. Finding the right house would have to be our first objective before we would put our houses up for sale.

Although finding the house and creating feasibility were major challenges, these issues gave me a chance to apply my thesis of scientific decision-making. When studying management at the Detroit College of Business in Dearborn, Michigan, I developed the following thesis if I were ever to pursue a doctorate's degree:

1. **Identify the problem.**
2. **Collect data.**
3. **Analyze and hypothesize.**
4. **Testing.**
5. **Application and review.**

Thus, we had to identify the problem or problems that would be confronting our marriage. How do we identify the problem? Ask questions. What kind of questions? Questions pertinent to the problem. The more pertinent is the question, the easier it is to identify the problem. Once we identified the problem, then we collected data. What kind of data? Well, of course, data pertinent to the problem.

One of the first question we faced was: How will the ten McMillan children get along with the seven Arsenault children? The data pertinent to this question could be collected at a family picnic with all the children. Together, Delores and I could carefully observe how the children got along. The date for the picnic was set and our two nine passenger station wagons were adequate to transport these seventeen children to the Huron Valley Park. Delores' two older boys were home from the seminary and were a great help with the smaller children. Even though Doc and Bob were fifteen and sixteen years old, they were excited about the picnic and were happy to attend. They were the goodwill ambassadors who acted as counselors and really showed their leadership abilities. I was quite surprised and delighted. This was the beginning of our scientific analysis.

The two station wagons with two adults and seventeen children converged on Huron River Park early on a Saturday morning in April. The weather was perfect for this special picnic where two anxious parents without partners watched carefully as the children were introduced to each other.

Since six of my children were the same age as six of Delores' children, and they seemed to pair up with their new friends, we could see that all was going well. Delores' four older boys were enjoying the games with all the younger children. Once again I recalled that old line from *Cheaper by the Dozen,* and I asked Delores "are these all our children or is this a picnic?"

She remembered the line as well and said, "Yes, these are all **our** children and believe me, *it's no picnic."*

We both laughed. But it really was a picnic and they really were our *fun* children.

Managers

It has been said that Americans are the best managers in the world and if three Americans ever got stranded on a desert island, they would immediately form a corporation…elect a president, secretary and treasurer. Then, they would call for a board meeting to discuss the problems. So it was with us. After the picnic, we had our board meeting and Delores and I discussed the results of the picnic under "old business." The analysis of the question of seventeen children getting along together was a tremendous success. In fact, they seemed to be very happy to have found new friends. Of course, this was only the first question tested. The question now was "would the harmony last?" We would need more…a lot more…observations and tests of the relationship between the children.

The next question asked under "new business" was: Where do we put seventeen children? I had a three-bedroom ranch home plus two more bedrooms with a bathroom in the finished basement for my three boys. This was a full house for seven children with parents. Delores had a colonial two-story home with four bedrooms and a large finished third-floor bedroom with a full bathroom and shower for her four older boys .A full house for a family of ten children and parents. Neither home would accommodate a family of nineteen. We would need to either expand one house by adding a couple more bedrooms and baths or buy a house that would already have enough bedrooms and baths. Delores' home was the only one that could be expanded.

Analysis: If we allocate two children per bedroom, we would need eight bedrooms for the children (one bedroom would have three children) and the ninth bedroom for the parents. Also, with nine bedrooms, we would need more than two bathrooms, perhaps even four or five bathrooms. The analysis of this data indicated that we needed to examine whether we could expand Delores' house or buy a new bigger house.

To test the hypothesis of expanding Delores' house, we had an architect draw up plans for a two-floor expansion attachment to the back of Delores' house. Her house was on a large lot that would accommodate such an addition. She also had a two-car unattached garage at the back of the lot to the right of the house that would not interfere with this addition. So for two hundred and fifty dollars, the architect drew up the blueprints and we submitted them to three local builders for cost estimates.

When the estimates came in, we found that the cost would be about the same as the value of the existing house, thus doubling the value of the house. We considered this to be too much money. That left us with the option to buy or build a new house. However, we still had the question: how much can we afford? Analysis: my house in Allen Park had a full mortgage. I had bought it under the *GI bill* with no money down. I had added a garage and some improvements but my estimated value would just pay off the mortgage and not leave much in addition. The real-estate market was, and had been, at a standstill for the past ten years. Delores' house had been paid off with her husband's insurance after his death, so we could put the full value of Delores' house as a down payment on a bigger home and our combined income would allow us to pick up the same amount as a mortgage, thus having doubled the value and size of Delores' house. This we could afford.

Then we asked: where are there large homes that have as many bedrooms and baths that we would need? Grosse Pointe Park had many large homes that would be adequate. Another place was *Grosse Ile*, the little island community about forty miles south of Detroit where the Detroit River empties into Lake Erie. We began checking for homes in Grosse Pointe Park and Grosse Ile for the size home we would need and for the price we could afford.

As we continued, we again realized that our marriage plan was not a simple decision and many questions still needed answering before we could make the move. We knew that *the house* was the biggest hurdle that we had to jump over. Love or no love, the order of business was now to find the *right* house before we could be married. Delores' *Novena* meant praying for the whole scheme, improbable, as it may have seemed. At times, we thought we would need a miracle. They say that 'love will find a way and pray for it.' And we did. We felt that the best marriages are *'made in heaven.'* The way things were going we wondered whether heaven was on our side. Well, the first sign of support from heaven would be...*the right house*.

IV

Fate or Destiny

A strict belief in fate is the worst kind of slavery; on the other hand there is comfort in the thought that God will be moved by our prayers.—Epicurus 342-270 BC

"I want some of my friends to meet you," Delores said with a twinkle in her eye. "I've been telling them about you for the last six months and so I'm planning a get together this week end. They're all anxious to meet you."

"Well, isn't that nice," I said. But I thought…I'd bet they're eager to meet me. They want to meet this guy who has seven kids and is willing to take on ten more children. Must be some kind of a nut. I could hear them now with their wise cracks like an old joke I remembered. "Do you know why God gives children to young people?"

"Because they don't know any better."

I anticipated their thoughts: "Here's a guy who doesn't know any better. Here's a guy, widowed, pushing forty, with seven children, engaged to a widow with ten children. I wonder what's wrong with his thinking?" I could hear them, "Why is he doing this?"

"It's an opportunity few men have!" I would answer.

"It's an opportunity few men want!" they would say.

"All it takes is good management," I would tell them.

"All it takes is dumb courage and blind faith," they would kindly reply.

"Wait a minute," I would counter, "put yourself in my place."

"Not on your life," they would say.

"Now wait," I would persist. "Let's be realistic and face the facts. Suppose you were left alone with seven or ten children...talk about Parents Without Partners. Don't you think that the job of raising all these children and providing for their needs in growing up would be easier for two experienced adults,...experienced working together, to manage than for each to be doing this parenting task alone? Consider two veterans, like Delores and myself: Don't you think that we, working together, could and would do a better job than if we had to do it alone? And besides, don't forget love. It takes a lot of love to raise a family and make a home for them. Delores and I love each other very much and we love our children. That should be worth something. By God, I know we can do it with God's help."

"You two had better learn how to pray a lot," they would say, "because you'll need a lot of God's help to make this work."

"But," I would say, "With God's help, we'll concede, all things are possible!"

"I'm afraid that you may need more than God's help and prayer."

"Sure, but remember, we're not just out of school you know. We're veterans in this parenting business, and if anyone can do it, we can."

Touché!

Tea For Two

Seventeen....what's so special about seventeen? Of course, if seventeen happens to be the number of your dependent children, well, that number takes on a whole new dimension.

Before I was married to Marge, I use to think that two children would be a good number for a family. Like the song, *Tea for Two*, "…a boy for you and a girl for me" would be good.

However, fate and time have a way of changing ideas. The Catholic Church stated that the main purpose of marriage was to procreate children. Well, that seemed all right with us as long as we were able to financially take care of these children. It's nice to believe that God knows what He's doing and He's in control and that it will all work out for the better. At least, I'd like to think that it would. But, at the age of thirty-nine, I found myself with seven children and soon to have seventeen. Over night, I would be adding eleven more dependents. Seemed hard to believe…father of seventeen children with the youngest three and the oldest, seventeen. If I were to be the father of seventeen children, then it behooves me to be the very best father that I can possibly be. All I had to do was to define *best* and pursue that course. However, *it's easier said than done* as the old saying so aptly puts it.

What occurrences in my upbringing, my youth, could have conditioned me and led me to this event? Did God or fate have anything to do with it? It's not probably. We make our own troubles. However, I believe that God is there to offer help along the way in all circumstances of our own making. What in my past could have conditioned me and prepared me for this stage of my life that I would contemplate and accept the obligation of being the father of seventeen children with some hope for success?

V

La Maison

Houses are built to live in more than to look at; therefore, let use be preferred to uniformity, except where both may be had.
—F. Bacon 1561-1625.

Getting married is not a simple matter when you have seventeen children of ages three to seventeen to contend with and you must assure for their welfare. There is not only the question of getting them into a school but because of our upbringing, it would have to be a Catholic school. Of my seven children, my three-year-old was with my mother and six were now attending St. Mary Magdalen's Catholic School in Allen Park. Delores' three-year-old was home and six children were attending St. Clare of Montefalco Parish School, one boy was attending the Augustinian Preparatory School for Boys in Detroit and the two older boys were at the Augustinian Seminary in Holland, Michigan. When we married, we would have fifteen children in school and two at home. That's twelve children in grade school, one in high school and two at the seminary. That's quite a bit to manage.

During the time we were resolving our unanswered issues, I was attending night school two days a week at the Detroit College of Business working to finish the requirements for my four-year Bachelor of Science degree in management. I was studying management decision-making and I tried to apply what I was studying to the issues we faced. I developed a thesis to solve these questions. It struck me that my personal issues were a lot like business problems. We needed to have a five-year plan and have a working budget or we could lose everything.

"Delores," I said, "finding a suitable house seems to be an impossible task. What if we consider keeping the two houses and, just for our analysis, let's consider this union of our new marriage as a business venture and run it like any business. As an accountant with General Motors, I know how to make a budget so that we will know exactly what kind of money we're talking about, what it will cost and we'll treat this union in marriage just like a business *joint venture*. We will operate just like GM."

"How can we do that?"

"Well, by using *POC,* the functions of management: *Plan, Organize and Control.* First, we will decentralize our operation by locations and we will designate managers for our two locations. We can delegate to our assigned managers the necessary authority and autonomy to operate two separate units, one east of Detroit and the other west of the city where they are already situated. Top management…you and I…will open a home office headquarters in downtown Detroit. We will be half way between the east side and west side…our two units of operations."

"Of course, you're kidding?"

"Sure. But it's fun just to suppose and think about it. Besides, just think of the possibilities: we could set up a controls by closed circuit TV; we could maintain both homes as is without any changes; we can have immediate communication by telephone; we can make daily visits to assure that we're not losing control."

"Sorry, George. I don't think that it will work. The cost of setting up another location would be too much. Secondly, children of all ages need constant supervision and delegating that much management responsibility to the older children is too much for any young person. No, George, you'll have to think of something else."

"Now that you mention it, I know that you're right about the cost factor. I know that when GM makes a move, they usually do it to increase their efficiency and reduce costs. We would be increasing our costs and reducing our efficiency. Yeah, you're right. It wouldn't work but it was fun to contemplate. I can think of three reasons why it wouldn't work: First, the cost would be too high. Secondly, the control would be too slow and difficult. And third, as you stated, the parents need to live with all the children."

Since adding on to Delores' house here in Grosse Pointe Park would be too expensive, we now were sure that purchasing a larger house was a better hypothesis than adding on to an existing house. Houses that are designed originally with six or seven bedrooms are better proportioned and having been built with cheaper labor costs is a better buy economically. The *add-on* hypothesis became a mute question.

One of our friends suggested a different proposal suggesting that we buy a small motel at the outskirts of the city. This was an interesting idea. Everyone would have a private room with a private bath and their own closet. We could have a large family room with kitchen for meals and recreation. The problem with this concept was that there were no reasonably priced small motels available in our price range or at a convenient and desirable location. Also, the overhead cost of heat would be too high and maintenance would be a full-time job. So, we quickly scrapped that idea. We were back to finding an existing large house.

We had considered building a new house, but the costs in subdivisions where new homes were being built was beyond our budget. The monthly mortgage payments we could afford indicated that we needed to look in older neighborhoods where prices were more within our reach.

"There has to be a used large house for sale somewhere that would accommodate our needs and would be within our budget," I said to Delores.

"But, George, I'm still not sure that we can afford the costs of buying a larger house and then maintain all the additional expenses of higher taxes and higher utility expenses."

"I've already made a budget and we're in good shape."

"Yes, I know. But, can we be sure we have anticipated all our costs including mortgage payments, property taxes and dozens of other costs?"

"Remember," I said, "there are many cost savings in our *joint venture*. As far as the other costs, that's where you come in. Check my lists of expenses and make sure I didn't miss something. Identifying all our expenditures is mandatory to our success. Let me put it this way. There are two kinds of costs that we have to consider, the same as General Motors or anyone else on a budget. Those costs are *fixed* and *variable*. The fixed costs are reoccurring costs that do not readily change, like insurance payments, property taxes and mortgage payments. These costs are not easily changed. Now, the variable costs are different. Things like food, clothing, recreation and other like expenditures can be changed easily. These costs we can do something about. We don't need a two or three thousand-dollar vacation every year. That's a variable cost that we can forgo to stay within our income and budget. We don't need to hire painters for our house. We can do the painting ourselves and save the money. That's a variable cost. So, there's a lot of ways we can stay within our budget. We don't need to eat at restaurants. We'll eat at home and save some more money."

"No more vacations on the French Riviera, I guess," Delores said with a laugh.

"Right. Now you have the idea. Budgeting is not easy. And a budget is a dynamic plan. It changes as you go and as you make certain value judgments and expenditure decisions. Another savings will be the wear and tear on my car not to mention the cost of gasoline for me driving every day from the west side to the east side."

"Also," Delores added. "Don't forget that my Social Security as a widow would come to a halt but the Social Security payments for the children will continue until they're out of school. So, that's a plus."

"We can also expect a large savings on income taxes with my putting in nineteen dependents," I added. "Variable costs, such as hamburger, hand-me-downs, and local vacations are already the order of the day."

"That sure sounds like a business. But what does it all mean?"

"It means," I said still trying to be business-like, "that we have a good hypothesis that indicates this merger can financially be feasible where all the costs are controlled and *if*. And here's a big *if*...if we can find *the house* that will have the necessary rooms and be within our budget for mortgage payments, insurance and property taxes."

"I think that both of our families moving into a new house is the best idea," Delores said. "That way when the question comes up with the children of whose house is this, it's not the Arsenault house or the McMillan house, everyone in the family can say, 'it's *our* house...my mom and dad just bought it...we just moved in.'"

"I totally agree," nodding my head in concurrence. At present, we have the *Arsenault house* and the *McMillan house*. That would change to *our house*."

"Then we agree that this would contribute to our goal of family unity and family *esprit de corps*. The house is not yours *or mine*...the house is *ours*. Our unity would be enhanced as we all become one family living in *our house* under equal and joint ownership."

So, the search for *la maison* continued through the winter of 1965 and into the spring of 1966. Months went by as we searched the papers every day with no luck. It was our thesis that God gave us all these children and He would prefer that they had both a father and a mother, who loved all of them dearly, and all lived in one home. Therefore, it follows that God will provide the necessary means to do this. After fifty-four days or almost two months of praying and searching, we finished the novena and we were still trying to find *the right house*.

The Family

What a family this will be. Imagine seventeen individual children with their unique personalities…all precious children…all living as one family in one house. Just for the record, the following is a list of names and birth dates, in chronological order:

1. Donald Robert McMillan — April 16, 1949
2. Robert James McMillan — June 27, 1950
3. Timothy John McMillan — May 14, 1951
4. Joseph Patrick McMillan — March 23, 1953
5. Mary Ann Arsenault — January 9, 1954
6. Patricia Marie McMillan — March 21, 1954
7. Patrick Joseph Arsenault — June 23, 1955
8. Ann Louise McMillan — October 16, 1955
9. Margaret Elizabeth Arsenault — Dec 16, 1956
10. Martin Dennis McMillan — April 5, 1957
11. Robert Ernest Arsenault — February 14, 1958
12. Mark Anthony Arsenault — March 10, 1959
13. Steven Thomas McMillan — July 3, 1959
14. Susan Jane McMillan — May 13, 1960
15. Aileen Therese Arsenault — July 22, 1960
16. Janet Frances Arsenault — November 8, 1962
17. Mary Ann McMillan — March 10, 1963

Everyone is a special person with a very unique and lovable personality. Everyone has his or her own story to tell. As we have always said, *"we wouldn't trade any one of them for a million dollars."*

VI

La Chateau

For a man's house is his castle.
—Sir Edward Coke 1552-1634.

Daily searching the newspapers for available houses and talking to real estate brokers seemed endless and futile. We spent our weekends driving around collecting data on large houses that were for sale in various communities. One day, when I was looking through the Detroit News classified ads, I came across a house with eight bedrooms. I called Delores to tell her the news.

"Delores, I found a house with eight bedrooms."

"Where?"

"On Grosse Isle."

"That's thirty miles from Detroit," Delores said. "Don't you think that that's a little bit too far from your work at Fisher Body Fleetwood in Detroit?"

"Not really with today's cars and good roads. We have a couple of people at Fleetwood that live on Grosse Isle. The head of the payroll department lives on Grosse Isle and he thinks it's great to get away from the big city. Another guy, an engineer, lives on the island and he says it's like being on vacation all year with the swimming, fishing, right at their doorstep. They call themselves *The Islanders*."

"Well, I suppose it wouldn't do any harm to go look at it. How much are they asking for it?"

"Right in our ballpark…around fifty thousand. I'll call the realtor and get some more information and make an appointment to see the house."

Grosse Isle

"This house is perfect for you and your family, Mr. Arsenault," the realtor said. "And it is available for immediate occupancy. The owner is a retired couple that lives in Florida. It has eight bedrooms and four baths on the second floor with a half bath on the first and in the basement. It's beautifully situated with lake frontage and a boat well right on the river leading out to Lake Erie. And the best news is that they will let it go for fifty thousand dollars. They were asking eighty thousand a year ago."

The price was within our planned budget so we made arrangements to see this eight-bedroom home on the waterfront

The Castle

Bright and early on a Saturday morning, I picked up Delores. We had 'ready made-live in' baby sitters so that we could go for a couple of hours. We drove west on the Ford Expressway to the interchange and took the Chrysler Expressway downtown to the I-75 Fisher Expressway…due

South…Driving downriver to Grosse Isle, we wondered just how *perfect* this house would be.

Arriving at the exit for the North River Bridge, we drove over the bridge onto the island to the Realtor's office. She was waiting at the door and motioned to us to park our car in the driveway. She drove us in her Cadillac and gave us a tour of the island before taking us to the *perfect* house. Almost all the roads were either gravel or dirt.

We drove across many small bridges crossing creeks, streams, and twisting in and out around the island. We drove across a small bridge and followed a dusty dirt road until we came to an old rusty iron gate across a driveway. The realtor stopped to open the gate and as we continued up the driveway, we had our first glimpse of the proposed house. I had the feeling that I had seen this place before…a large foreboding three-story house sitting atop a small mound…but where?

"This place reminds me of some place I've already seen," I whispered to Delores. " Now I remember…all we need is some thunder and lightning. It's Dracula's Castle."

It was big all right. The house was situated on an acre of land surrounded by trees and shrubs. Everything was overgrown and unkempt. All the rooms were very large. I seemed to feel a draft going up the main staircase from the entrance hall with its large fireplace. Plenty of dollars to heat this place, I thought. The ceilings were at least ten feet high. I could just see our heating bills in the winter with the dollars flying out the window. The place needed a lot of repair, both mechanical and structural. The walls in all the rooms needed paint and the cracks needed repair. There were even signs of water leaks in some rooms. "Does the roof leak?" I asked the realtor pointing to the ceiling in the master bedroom.

"Yes, the roof does need repairing. But, I already have a contractors estimate for that repair," she said. "I'll give you a copy when we get back to the office. But this house is a handyman's dream.

We went down to the basement where we found a very large room at the foot of the basement stairway, which was finished with a hard wood floor. It had a door going outside and there was a stairway leading to the back yard. Another door from this 'recreation' basement room led to a hallway with smaller rooms attached. Down at the end of the hallway there was a door leading to the furnace room and the laundry room. I looked at the furnace and it was an old coal burning steam boiler that had been converted to oil. Next to the boiler was a large 200-gallon oil tank.

"It's a great investment to make some money in the future," the realtor suggested.

"I'll bet it is," but not for us I thought. The longer we toured this empty house, the more it supported my first impression that this is not the right house.

The price was so reasonable because the house had not been lived in for more than a year and it was run down and the area was run down.

Thanks, but no thanks. We scratch *Dracula's Castle off our list*.

VII

The House

The first indication of domestic happiness is the love of one's home.
Frances D. Montlosier 1755-1838.

In the spring of 1966, we were still looking for a house. The world was still going around the sun. That year, *The Man of La Mancha* was named New York's Drama Critics 'Best Musical' where the song *The Quest* was sweeping Broadway off its feet and Delores and I were still pursuing our *quest* for the *impossible dream*.

One day, while driving down some streets in Grosse Pointe Park looking for new *for sale* signs, I noticed a large home just off Jefferson Avenue on Devonshire Road. It had overgrown shrubbery around it and a large hedge across the front of the house. In the hedge was a *for sale* sign. When I arrived at Delores' house on Balfour, I told her about this home and we decided to go take a look at it.

Our first impression was that it would be large enough for our needs. The address was *one thousand*. "Nice address," I said to Delores. "I like the Mediterranean design with a center entrance. Notice how the sun golden bricks with a *Gothic* style of rounded arches for the doors and windows give the house an air of the Mediterranean Riviera. It also has a slate roof. That type roof will last a hundred years."

The house also had a grape arbor walkway with roman white pillars supporting large wooden crossbeams over the walkway. The arbor walkway started at a screened-in porch at the side of the house facing the vacant attached lot and ends after about forty feet into a large tiled patio with a picnic table sheltered by large fir trees around it. The adjacent lot was filled with fruit trees and shrubs much like a park. Next to the screened-in porch was a flower conservatory complete with a water fountain and glass skylight dome.

"Delores," I said. "Call the realtor tomorrow and find out what they want for this place and make an appointment for us to see it."

"I'll call in the morning. But, I wonder why we haven't seen the for sale sign before. We've been up and down these streets for more than four months now. Can you imagine that *the* house was only a few blocks from my house on Balfour? It looks like the perfect house for our family, but can we afford their price? "

For Sale Again

"Your timing is perfect," the realtor said, " because the house had been sold but since the buyer's mortgage was not approved, the deal fell through. The house just went back on the market this week. Call this number for an appointment with the owners and the owners son or daughter show you around."

"Can you tell me what the price is that they are asking for the house?" Delores asked.

"I know that they had sold it for eighty thousand dollars, but that included thirty thousand for the vacant lot next to it on the corner. She might sell it without the lot for fifty thousand."

When Delores told me about the house and the price, I said, "Bingo! The pieces are starting to fall in place. Will wonders ever cease? "

Touring The House

Delores made an appointment to see the house for the next evening. The owner's daughter said she would be glad to show us around. That evening, we walked up to the front door at exactly six o'clock. The owner's daughter opened the door and invited us into the house. The front door had a large brass handle and the door was rounded at the top. It was solid wood about three inches thick. The entrance was a small marble floor with an equally heavy oak door on each side of the front door leading to two closets. A second door led out of the entrance hall into the lobby where a large staircase led to the upstairs. The entrance alone was very impressive. The realtor had said that the house has about six thousand square feet with nineteen rooms.

"How many bedrooms are there?" I asked

"There are seven bedrooms and four bathrooms on the second floor. We have two master bedrooms with tub and stall showers. The largest is the main master bedroom. It has a dust balcony, with French doors, overlooking the back-yard patio and a walk-in dressing room closet. Then off the hallway on the second floor, there's a six-by-eight foot walk-in linen closet and a five-by-eight foot walk-in cedar closet."

Touring the first floor, we found a large kitchen with a butler's pantry and a large breakfast room. We then went into a very large dining room with a fireplace at the far end where a leaded glass door led out to a screened-in porch and patio. We continued into the large living room through a sliding door. The living room had a beautiful stone carved fireplace. At the far end of the living room was another leaded glass door to a small conservatory with a glass dome and a fountain with water squirting into a large gold fish pool. The living room and the dining room also both had leaded glass French doors leading into the main entrance room. Down the hall from the entrance room, we were led into the mahogany book cased library room and further down the hall were a half bathroom and a door leading outside to the driveway.

We went down to see the basement using the beautiful front stairway just off the library that was papered with scenes of Paris. There were four large rooms in the basement. One room was fourteen feet by forty-five feet called the "ballroom" that had a hardwood floor and a fireplace. There was even a small bar room attached to the ballroom. Using the back stairway up to the kitchen, we continued up to the second floor and a stairway to the third floor. On the third floor was a very large room that measured about fifty-six feet long and twenty-five feet wide with a very high ceiling under the roof. In my mind, I imagined it to be finished into two large rooms.

Descending to the second floor, we saw the seven bedrooms with four bathrooms. There was a long hallway with a full bath and two bedrooms. This must have been the servants' quarters with these two bedrooms and their own bathroom at the end of this hallway. At the far end of the hallway was a door. Passing through this door and turning left was another long hallway with the grand front staircase about half way down. At the head of the staircase was the master bedroom. It had its own dressing room with bath and stall shower as we had been told. At the start of the hallway was a second bedroom that had its own private bath and stall shower. Down at the far end were two more bedrooms that shared a bathroom between them with each having its own entrance door from their room. At the end of the main hallway, there was another door leading to another room with large windows facing southeast. Our *tour guide* said that this was called the sunroom. On this floor there was also the large walk-in linen closet and a walk-in cedar closet. At the head of the large winding staircase were two French doors leading to a small room with a kneeling bench and a religious icon. This room was used as a chapel, the daughter told us.

The house had three fireplaces...one in the large living room, one in the large dining room, and one in the ballroom in the basement. The house had a four-car attached garage with electronic operating door openers. The garage was set sideways at the back of the house and could not be seen from the front of the house. There was a door to a large attached screened in porch adjacent to the grape arbor walkway that lead to the patio with a picnic table. The dining room also had two French doors leading directly out into another patio adjacent to the screened in porch.

We spent more then an hour and a half just walking through the house. There were so many things of interest to see, like the conservatory with its fountain and skylight ceiling, the dust porch with its French doors with a view of the park-like back yard and the master bedroom with the adjacent sunroom. The screened in back patio, the butler's pantry with its own sink, and the library with a half bathroom next to it was very appealing. There were seven doors leading to the outside from the first floor. There were even two basement doors leading out to the back yard.

As we left and I opened the door of the car for Delores, I said, "This could be the perfect house for us, Delores. Did you like it?"

"I loved it. You're right, this could be the answer to our prayers."

"If we can swing the deal, we could be married in a month or two for the closing since we will have to be married in order to jointly sign the papers together as man and wife. Doesn't that sound nice? Man and wife."

"Just keep praying," Delores said. "Whatever will be, will be."

"We're sure are busy praying. I had never said a 54-day novena before. I didn't even know that they had these long novenas. I always thought they were only seven days. Well, when all else fails, keep praying, you and some saint said."

VIII

Planning

Not failure, but low aim, is a crime.
J. R. Lowell 1819—1891.

When I was a nine year old, my father died. Without a father, I remember I felt like a "second class citizen." Many times, I wished I had a father around like everyone else in my school, somebody to go home to and talk to every day. I surely missed my dad as I went through grade school and high school. I was in the third grade when my dad died. So, I knew that it's not easy for children to grow up with only one parent. My mother was a saint. I don't know how she managed to keep the family together. She sure knew how to stretch a dollar and make ends meet. But, I remember thinking that it would have been nice to know that I could take my problems to either one of two parents as most of my friends. It's nice if there are two parents to help children when they needed a helping hand as they grow up. One parent alone with the burden of raising children is a heavy responsibility of making all the decisions in planning, organizing, and control of children.

Later, after leaving the Army, when I was still young and before I was ever married, I use to think: To be average is a desirable goal. The average man does pretty well for himself in this great American land of plenty. He lives a pretty good life working eight hours a day and five days a week. He eats three meals a day and has his home and a car to drive around. He pays his taxes and takes a vacation every year. My dad died at age 42, the average man lives to about 65.

Yes, the average man lives a pretty good life, so if I can be average, that's better than my dad and I'll be satisfied with average." That was my thesis for the good live.

But, when Marge died, and I was left alone with seven children, all under twelve years old, and I was without their mother to help me raise them. Well, that's not average! Therefore, I thought to myself, if fate won't allow me to be average, then by God, I'm going to start being better than average…not less. That's why, when Marge died, I decided to go back to college and get my degrees. I decided that my new desire for more education would be based on a new axiom: *you can always do more than you think you can.*

I made many plans to change things and try to make something positive out of the disaster caused by her death. However, little did I realize that two years later there would be ten more children? Going back to college was also partially an escape mechanism to take my mind off of my torments. But, this continued education took on a greater significance when fate presented me with this new role as the father of seventeen children. I felt that it behooved me to continue the pursuit of that bachelor's degree as an example of the importance of education for my children. Now, even more than ever, I thought, I might also continue onto a master's degree. I set my aim to a higher goal. My aim was to be the best father these children would ever want.

Thus these plans for higher education and my endeavors to learn more would help me meet my obligation to be the best father possible. If my thesis on education was correct before, it was even more correct now. For example, even though I no longer needed the therapeutic value of study that I may have needed two years ago, I now felt that I should aspire to a better paying job just to support my large family with all the many additional bills.

Teamwork

The belief that God gives us talents and it's up to us to develop those talents and give them back to God a hundred fold is a biblical teaching. It's in the Bible someplace. I felt that to be the best father I would need all the help I could get from education and God. And, since my studies were in management and administration, I felt that these subjects would be very valuable to our success in this *joint venture* of marriage. We could put the things I learned to practical use right at home. But more importantly, I was lucky to have Delores, who was an able and wise homemaker and manager, willing and happy to manage the home with seventeen children while I would be attending classes two to three nights a week. This was just one more reason for me to endeavor even harder. Delores made all the difference in the world. Teamwork is the key. Success is easier with two working together in this crazy mixed up world. Another axiom: *behind every good man there's a better woman.*

It's a big job for two people and much more for one person alone. Many can't cope with it. They end up with nervous breakdowns or, worse, they take to drinking and become alcoholics. The children are the big losers. They not only suffer the loss of a parent but they are sometimes left to shift for themselves in this world that turns cold against them. Yes, the job of raising a family is much easier when there are two loving parents working together. So, getting married to a widow with ten children was an opportunity for me to pursue happiness for others. It was my privilege and honor, especially when it was this woman and these children.

IX

Marriage:
The Second Time Around

> *Were a man not to marry a second time,*
> *It might be concluded that his first wife*
> *Had given him a disgust for marriage; but*
> *By taking a second wife, he pays the highest*
> *Compliment to the first by showing that she*
> *Made him so happy as a married man that*
> *He wishes to be so a second time.*
> Samuel Johnson—1709-1784

I think marriage is God's way of forcing us to think of somebody else and taking our minds off ourselves. Children are God's way of further forcing us to continue to think of others and to further stop thinking of ourselves. I think that happiness is doing something for somebody else. The ego and the id are very poor companions in this journey through life that we find ourselves in this world. They can cause us a lot of unhappiness and stress. They even can destroy us if we let them. So, I think that the most important thing to do when you're sad is to *do something for somebody quick. A*nd that's what fate did for me after my devastation. It forced me to change my focus from myself to others. I think that "fate" and "god" are in close proximity.

X

The Wedding

I read the newspapers to see how God governs the world.
John Newton 1801-1890

My brother in-law, Patrick J. Foley, the brother of my first wife, Marge, was our attorney in the sale of our existing houses and the purchase of our pending new home. Pat called me a few days after we had signed the purchase agreement on the house at 1000 Devonshire.

"George," Pat said. "I just got word from the realtor that the owners have changed their mind and they are withdrawing the purchase agreement."

"They can't do that," I said. "What are they talking about?"

"They're talking about attempting to get out of the deal and not sell you the house."

"They can't do that," I repeated. They signed the purchase agreement."

"Yes, you're right. But, they're trying to break the contract if we let them."

"Well, we're not going to let them. This is the perfect house for the seventeen and I'm not going to spend another six months looking again."

"That's what I thought you'd say," Pat agreed. "But I wanted to hear it from you first."

"Why do they want to renege now, two weeks before the wedding?"

"I don't really know for sure. But, I have a suspicion that they received a better offer by someone else that would buy the house and the vacant lot next door. In short the answer is more money!"

"Well, it's too late. Tell them *no way!* They can sell the lot but not the house. The house is already sold to us."

"OK, I'll take care of it," Pat said as he hung up the phone.

The owner had been trying to sell the house and the lot together. We had offered to buy the house alone. The corner lot was priced at about forty percent of the cost of the house. We could only afford to buy the house as we had planned in our budget analysis. We didn't need the lot. We did need the house.

A few days later, Pat Foley called back and said, "Well, the deal is on again. The owners are going to go through with the purchase agreement and sell you the house to you as agreed. "

"How did you manage to convince them?"

"Easy! I just told their lawyer that when we walk into court, I will have seventeen children following me into the courtroom."

"That was all you said?"

"Yes! That was all I said. It took all the fight out of him. He knew he had no chance."

"All right! Nice job, Pat. Keep up the good work."

Preparations

Preparation for our wedding included outfitting the two families in their Sunday best. That called for a "full dress *class A"* uniform inspection, referring back to my army days, and review by the commanding officers, Delores and me. After checking the seventeen for suits, blazers, shoes and dresses we began to issue the necessary attires. Delores volunteered to sew all the girls' new dresses. These dresses were to be *hand-made* and not *homemade* by Delores. Hand-made implies the skill of a seamstress, whereas, homemade implies the product of an amateur. Luckily, Delores was a talented accomplished seamstress among her other talents, so the new dresses were perfect.

One family with nineteen members led to what I call a multiple *progression* phenomenon. Everything from now on would have to be considered in multiples. We could not buy one child a present without buying all seventeen children a present. The budget cost of anything and everything would have to stand the test of *multiple progressions* in our budget. This phenomenon of multiplicity would reoccur over and over again in the months and years to come. But, one of the rewards was that our happiness as a family would also be multiplied. This was an advantage that the children would always cherish as time went by.

June 10, 1966

The date for the wedding was set for Friday morning, June 10, 1966. Father Sweeney, the pastor of St. Clare of Montefalco Church in Grosse Pointe Park, would say the mass. We chose Friday for the wedding so that we could have the weekend for the honeymoon trip and I would use the minimum amount of vacation time from work.

We also chose June 10 because we had the all-important closing date for the house six days later. This gave us five days for our planned honeymoon trip to Canada. We could not jointly get a mortgage for the new house until we were man and wife. Thus, the closing requirements for purchasing with the new bank mortgage had to be preceded by our wedding.

It was eight o'clock in the morning of our wedding day when I received a phone call at my house in Allen Park. It was a reporter from the Detroit News. Someone had called them and told them that Delores and I were getting married this morning. They wanted to verify the facts about the wedding and the circumstances. I later was told by Dick Wolff, a very good friend of Delores, that he had told his brother, Joe Wolff, a journalist at the Detroit News about the wedding. I guess that when a man and women take on seventeen young children, that's news.

The morning of our wedding was a beautiful, bright and sunny day. No wonder a lot of people have their weddings in June. The perfect month for our wedding…it was not too hot and not too cold, just right. If the start of our wedding day was any omen, we could expect a beautiful and happy future for our family. I even heard the birds singing and the flowers were never more beautiful…blossoms everywhere.

June rhymes with moon, spoon, and tune. June has the most sunny days and mild weather. It's so nice to have this beautiful weather after a long winter. And, like the song says…*just when your poor old heart can't go on, it seems; June brings a basket full of dreams.* And, that was what we had on our wedding day. We had a basket full of dreams.

St. Clare De Montefalco

As we had arranged, I drove my children to Delores' house on the morning of the wedding and after the final inspection, we would all get into our two station wagons and drive to St. Clare De Montefalco Church for the wedding. Delores and I had our hands full making sure that everyone was presented at their best for the mass. The children were all excited with anticipation. Participation in the wedding ceremony included all 19 of us as Delores had planned. When Delores' sister, Patricia, asked our two three-year olds, "Who's getting married this morning?" Little Mary Ann McMillan and little Janet Arsenault both answered, "we are! All of us."

They were right. We were all getting married. One big happy wedding makes one big happy family. That was our prayer. This was a storybook wedding. This was a wedding where the bride and groom's children would all be in the wedding and they would all participate, each one marching down the aisle to the front of the church just as Delores had planned it. We wanted unity and togetherness and it would start right from the beginning. It would not be *your children and my children*. It would be *our children*. They would all be *our children* right from the beginning.

Delores' four older boys, Donald, Bob, Tim and Joe, seventeen, sixteen, fifteen and fourteen respectively, would be on the altar assisting Father Sweeney in the Mass ceremony while the two seven-year-old look alike, Susan McMillan and Aileen Arsenault, were the flower girls. All the rest preceded us down the center aisle. All the children were dressed up in their best. Many had new shoes and all had something new. It was quite a glamorous showing.

Notoriety

All morning long, at my house in Allen Park and at Delores' house in Grosse Pointe Park, the newspaper reporters kept calling and asking questions. "Is it true that you're getting married? Is it true that there are seventeen children between you? Is it true that you are joining two families to make a family of nineteen?" Now, in front of the church as we were going in for the ceremony, there they were, still asking questions but talking to our friends and relatives. They were talking to everyone it seemed. We had taken a low profile approach to the news media for the children's sake. But it seemed that everyone was interested in our *joint venture.*

The wedding ceremony went like clock work as Delores' careful planning paid off, one more indication of her talent as a great manager and organizer. As the last of the children were sent up the center aisle ahead of us, Delores said, with a twinkle in her eye, "I'm not going through with it. I've changed my mind."

"Delores," I said. "I hope you're kidding?"

"Yes, I'm kidding," as she took my arm and started us down the center aisle.

All went well without a hitch as we promised to *love one another until death do us part.* Everyone did his or her part in the wedding and we tied the knot firmly. After the ceremony, we all gathered on the steps in front of the church. The photographers were snapping our pictures before, during, and after the ceremony. My brother, Albert, and Delores' brother, Bob Shmina, were busy with their cameras taking pictures of the occasion. We had *stills* and *home movies* to remember the day. We also had the reporters and their photographers taking pictures as all nineteen members of this new Arsenault-McMillan family were exiting the church. Standing on the steps of the church together, the photographers were directing us to move over or stand here or there as they focused their cameras around us.

Little did we realize that the Detroit News and the Detroit Free Press would have our picture and story on their front pages the very next day, big as life!

All the papers and the Associated Press picked up the picture and the story. We later discovered that we made the newspapers from New York to Florida. We even received a clipping of our picture and story from a Texas newspaper. "All the world's a stage," I thought. When I was driving to Grosse Pointe, the car radio played songs like *People, Strangers in the Night* and *Follow Your Dream* from the popular movie *The Sound of Music*. I felt that this was omen and I thought that this *joint venture* is bound to work. Everything seems to point us in that direction. I felt that this was more of the writing on the wall. To add to the positive signs, while our family pictures was being taken on the front steps of the church, we were told that Delores' dad and mother were discussing with each other that with Delores' new additional seven children, they would now have thirty five grandchildren. It was nice to hear such positive remarks and acceptance by the grandparents.

The plan for our honeymoon was to stay overnight in downtown Detroit at the then new Pontchartrain Hotel. The next morning, we would drive to Toronto, Canada where we would stay overnight and then fly to Montreal leaving our car at the airport.

When we arrived in Montreal, my cousin, Gilberte Bujold, told us she saw our picture on their evening television news. Needless to say, we felt like celebrities as a result of all this publicity. In Montreal, we made a short visit to my two aunts who were nuns at the convent house of the teaching Sisters of the Holy Cross. Aunt Lydia and Aunt Estelle (sisters of my mother) were delighted. They assured us that the children and we were in their prayers. Then, after a day of visiting, we took a train out of Montreal to Toronto and pick up our car at the airport after staying overnight at the airport motel.

The following day, we drove to the boarder crossing over the bridge to Buffalo on the American side and on to Cleveland for another overnight stay in Cleveland. The following day was Wednesday when we would drive home in time for the closing. We had to be home by Thursday to sign the papers as 'man and wife' for our new home. Actually, we were anxious to get home to the family. There were so many things for us to do, most of all the planning and preparing for the big move.

XI

Implementation

Where we cannot invent, we may at least improve.
Charles Colton 1780-1832

"Where would nineteen people sleep in one house?" That was the question of the day. We had designated the four main bedrooms in the front of the house as the girls' rooms, two in each bedroom. Delores and I would have the large master bedroom with our own bath. The oldest two girls would share the smaller master bedroom with its own bath and stall shower. Although the house had seven bedrooms and four full baths on the second floor, two of the bedrooms along the north wing section were originally servants' rooms or maids' quarters with a bath at the end of the hall, but the bedrooms were small and hardly enough room for nine boys. The servants' quarters had a door separating it from the rest of the house.

Luckily, the third floor was just as large as the second floor and also with high ceilings so we were able to build two large dormitory bedrooms for the nine boys. For the first month, they would bunk in the servants' quarters until we had finished putting up installation and paneling, complete with doors, hallway, and lighting on the third floor. The nine boys couldn't wait for it to be finish so that they would have more room. The five younger boys, Patrick Arsenault, Marty McMillan, Mark Arsenault, Steve McMillan, and Robert Arsenault would share one of two large room

(17' x 25') and the four oldest boys, Donald, Robert, Timothy, and Joe (all McMillans), would share the other large room. Each room had a built in desk with light for studying. The four older boys had a large closet and the five younger boys each had footlockers and an open clothes closet. These were the plans.

But, the city building inspector told me that he would not approve the construction plans for third floor occupancy until we put in a fire escape from the third floor. There were two windows on the third floor, one in each new room. At the furthest window from the stairway, we installed a thirty-foot chain escape ladder that was bolted to the windowsill and unfolded out to the ground. We made a 8mm home movie demonstrating the unfolding and use of this emergency exit. The two oldest boys, Donald, and Bob McMillan, were the stars of this movie and did the honors of demonstrating the ladder's use. Strict orders were given that this ladder would be used only in an emergency. Hopefully, it would never be used. Because of our limited budget, the family except for the electrical revisions and modernization of the kitchen did all the work. Delores' father A. Z. Shmina & Sons donated the insulation of the third floor.

The kitchen renovation resulted after identification of the problems by asking such questions as: How does one feed nineteen people every day? Who does the planning and cooking? Who will do the cleanup after each meal? Do we have the right tools in the kitchen to do the job? Although the house was in very good condition, the house was forty years old and the kitchen somewhat antiquated. It had a very large industrial size gas stove made of iron. There was a very old canopy vent over the stove that dominated the kitchen. There was a sink in the main kitchen and a small sink in the butler's pantry, a room next to the kitchen. Each sink had a window over it. The butler's pantry had cabinets for dishes on both sides of the room. We felt that since the kitchen would be of prime importance every day and Delores' main work area, it should be modernized with all the latest conveniences. The old kitchen was not very functional for our purposes and therefore all approved the proposal for a new kitchen. A plan to refurbish and modernize the kitchen was solicited from a contractor. Mutschler Kitchens, of Grosse Pointe, was called on to do the job. It had a good reputation around Grosse Pointe of being the best and had been recommended to us. We would use the money we received for our wedding to start the job. The plan called for the replacement of the old refrigerator, stove, and sinks with new fixtures that would include a new refrigerator, double electric ovens, plus an electric range and a large microwave oven.

This new kitchen would have a built-in range with double self-cleaning ovens, built-in large capacity dishwasher, and refrigerator with a large freezer compartment. The basement would also have a refrigerator, a freezer cabinet, and a stove salvaged from our old homes. The butler's pantry would be refurbished with a partial wall removal to form an island for the stove and double oven and a bar with four stools that would serve four children. Next to the kitchen was the large breakfast room. This room would easily accommodate the remaining fifteen persons at its long breakfast table. The table had five chairs on one side and six chairs on the other side plus two chairs at each end of the table. Fifteen would sit at the main table for dinner and four would sit at the bar. The ones at the bar would be those that were late, volunteers or those that were designated for infractions of the rules and paying their penalty. Since two of our boys would be in the seminary, only two need be at the bar.

It was a hard and fast rule from the very beginning that all would assemble for the daily main meal and all would eat together. This main event at the end of each day would allow us all to share the day's experiences. It would facilitate the daily review of the pertinent plans and problems listed under old and new business. It was our method of communication at this informal family meeting. All were members of the *board* and were expected to attend. We had strict rules about all of the family being present and on time for the evening meal. Delores would plan preparations early in the day. Evening dinner was a symbol of family unity. Favorite dishes, some taking many hours to cook, were brought to the table steaming hot. Delores liked everything piping hot.

The evening dinner was more than just a good time to enjoy good food; it was an occasion to share the day's events and to talk about the things that mattered most to the family. This was the occasion and time that we would plan annual vacations or other outings. This was a time to laugh at someone's silly jokes and offer suggestions to solve someone's special problems. It was a time to be together in a very special way that would benefit all the family.

Delores was the chief cook and homemaker. On our income tax returns, she was designated under the caption *occupation* as a *homemaker*. *Not* a housewife, her job was a *homemaker*. This was very important. She made it her job to plan each day's meals and to prepare each day's dinner to be served promptly at 6 p.m. She delegated tasks to everyone in the family. The eight girls would share in the serving and cleanup after the meal. Delores' plan worked very well. The girls paired off and each pair would take turns at different tasks. The boys would be responsible for maintaining the grounds outside, both winter and summer. Sections of the outside were assigned to each from a partitioning map of the areas.

Most of the meals were baked, broiled, or boiled. There was very little frying. Meat loaves, meatballs, hamburger patties, spaghetti, chicken, our butcher's city-chicken, and his mock chicken were especially liked. Baked hams and roast beefs with mashed potatoes were among the favorites meals. The roast beef, mashed potatoes and gravy were always a big winner.

When we were planning our wedding, Fisher Body Fleetwood was modernizing its kitchen at the plant. When I found out that they were going to replace all the equipment and fixtures, I called the Salvage Department at General Motors and asked if I could buy the meat slicer. When they heard about the seventeen children, they saw to it that I got the slicer. It was this butcher's slicer that made it easy to serve nineteen people roast beef or ham. I could slice it as thin as I wanted and we were always able to make it go around. Another favorite was Delores' beef barley soup. She did wonders with six pounds of ground beef. Six pounds meant quarter-pounders for everyone and some left over for seconds.

Steaks

We rarely had steak for dinner…not only because of the expense but also because of the difficulty in preparing nineteen steaks. However, once, my brother gave us a box of frozen steaks for a family treat. The children were all excited and let out the word in the local neighborhood that the Arsenault/McMillans were having steak for dinner tonight. Everyone, up and down the block, knew that George and Delores with their seventeen children would be having steak for dinner that night. As it turned out, the steaks were very tough. The children were busy trying to cut, chew, and swallow their steaks. They started to ask, "Is this steak?"

"Yes, this is steak. Do you like it?"

"No, I don't like it."

"Neither do I," one after the other said.

We had very few requests for steak after that experience. In fact, there are some of the children who today, many years later, still do not like steak. They would rather have hamburger than steak.

Saturdays and Sundays were days off for the chief cook and homemaker. So, it was *catch as catch can* for all. We always had cereal, milk, water, soups, sandwiches, and leftovers for everyone. The rule was: Eat when you're hungry but don't leave a mess.

We also tested the idea whether buying a half a cow for the freezer in the basement would be more economical. We discovered that cattle sold for freezers are usually a better grade and therefore, cost a little more than super market meat on sale. Also, there are many steaks and only a few roasts. We had the steaks ground into hamburger but that made our hamburger rather costly.

After our experience with one half a cow, we decided that it was more economical to buy our hamburger and roasts from the super market or a local butcher when they had sales. We found a butcher who knew about the seventeen children and he would tell us about his special sales. The lesson we learned from all this was that those who want top grade steaks and lots of convenience from shopping for meat could freeze a *half a cow* but it will cost them a little more and they will eat more meat. Our way was less expensive and less meat.

Bread

Another item on which we were able to save money but still have quality was bread. We estimated that we would use about five loaves a day. Bread came in twenty-sliced loaves and if we had seventeen sandwiches for the school lunches that would add up to 34 slices of bread. Many would take two sandwiches and we used up three loaves of bread for lunches. The daily ritual included the school milk money for fifteen plus, Delores would insist, each lunch must also include a piece of fruit and a cookie. Breakfast and dinner would also require bread and we used up another two loaves, if not more. Therefore, the *multiple progression phenomenons* were at work again. That also meant that we could use up to fifty loaves of bread every ten days.

    I located a Silver Cup bakery on the east side of Detroit on Chene and Mack Avenue and they would sell *surplus bread* every day at a discount. I would pass Chene on East Jefferson every day on my way to and from work at the GM Fleetwood Plant. Many times, I was able to buy as much as seven loaves for a dollar. Normally, I would only get four loaves for a dollar. Our freezer in the basement would hold about fifty loaves of bread. So, I would buy fifty loaves every ten days. I believe the freezer bread was even fresher when thawed than bread not frozen.

When we were low on cereal, toasted *bread* would be the choice. Sometimes, Delores would make French toast and we would use up more bread. Delores had a counter in the kitchen that she had designated for the school lunches. Every evening, prior to a school day, Delores would place three rows of napkins, six columns across on this counter. The school milk money was placed on each napkin. An apple or a piece of fruit was added with a napkin and a paper bag. This was the routine that Delores prepared each night before school. In the morning, the older girls had the task of making the sandwiches. There would be special orders for bologna or peanut butter and jam, or some other lunchmeat. The sandwiches were made on a production-line method where one would put the bread down; another would deal out the lunchmeat, mustard, lettuce and etc. On some occasions, there would be complaints that they got the wrong lunchmeat or no lunchmeat at all. Those complaints were sent to the complaint department and the management took it up with the workers…encouraging them to improve their quality controls.

Milk

Milk was another important item. How much milk do we need? And, where do we buy the milk? This was before 'skim' and '2%' milk and the time when everyone was talking about too much fat in milk. Milk was necessary for morning cereal. Cereal was a good nutrient and vitamin supplier and it had a low per serving cost factor but it required milk. Delores discovered powdered milk. Borden's powdered milk was the big rage to cut down the fat in milk. However, nobody liked the taste of powdered milk. Delores solved this problem by using one gallon of whole milk and one gallon of powdered milk. Mixing it together and you had the lower fat content and the taste was great. So, we would buy two gallons of whole milk and mix them with two gallons of watered powdered milk. Thus we would have four gallons of 'low fat' milk. Also, Delores decided that at the main meal, water would be served and not milk. This helped everyone to drink more water based on the medical advice that the average person should drink ten glasses of water a day.

Many more questions in our search to identify problems needed asking, such as, "who does the washing?" and "who does the shopping?" or "how do you keep track of seventeen children?" We searched for answers but, since all the members of the family were eager to make a success of this venture and all were working to help in any way that they could, we were confident that these and other questions, would be satisfactorily answered and *domestic tranquility* and happiness would prevail in our new *blue heaven*.

XII

Numbers

> *The heavens themselves, the planets, and this centre, observe degree, priority, and place, course, proportion, season, form, office, and custom, in all line of order.*
> —Shakespeare 1564-1616.

The rights and privileges of each family member are no small matters when they involve a family of seventeen children. After careful study and analysis, we decided that the ruling factor for rights and privileges would be seniority. Since the parents had the most seniority, they would be the managers. We would try to rule much like Socrates' *philosopher king* and thus wisdom and knowledge, derived from study and experience, would be given priority. Many questions such as: Who sits where at the table? Who sits next to the window in the car?; Who drives the car?; Who is in charge when the parents are away?; would be answered by *seniority*. The unions at GM and other companies use seniority to solve all types of problems and we felt it would work for us. Seniority allowed us to be fair to all.

Donald McMillan was the oldest and he became number one in seniority among the children. Everyone could count off his or her number in rank by seniority. Little Mary Ann McMillan, our three year old, was number seventeen. The school lunches and clean laundry were sorted 1 to

17. Clean laundry would be folded and put into 17 piles on a large table near the two washing machines and dryers. Delores took our own washing up to our room. But the children were expected to pick up their "piles" and take them to their rooms, putting them away in their closets and drawers. For the school lunches, one kitchen counter was used for setting up the lunches the night before. Since Bob and Donald McMillan were away at school, five columns and three rows of napkins and milk money would start the lunches for the next day. Sandwiches were made in the morning by Delores' helpers and place at the appropriate place. It was an easy way to identify who ordered the peanut butter sandwich and who got the bologna sandwiches.

This numbering system facilitated all communications. The main telephone was a wall-phone in the kitchen. When calls came in for any of the boys who were usually on the third floor, we would have to send someone up to get them. The nine boys were usually on the third floor where they studied, read, slept, and calling up to the third floor every time someone got a call was a problem. It was difficult to tell someone on the third floor that they had a call on the first floor. Also, when supper was served, the message had to go to the third floor for all the boys. We decided that we would install a buzzer on the third floor, which was activated in the kitchen. The main laundry chute, about two feet square, came down from upstairs and a door in the kitchen opened to this laundry chute which was right next to the wall phone. We ran a wire up to the third floor inside this laundry chute. Whenever calls for the boys came in, all we had to do was open the laundry chute door and buzz them by number.

The buzzer facilitated our communications for the boys on the third floor. In fact, you could hear these buzzes all over the house including the basement because of the laundry chute. We used a 1 to 9 numbering system for the nine boys. The oldest of the boys was number one and the youngest, Steven, was number nine. Luckily, most of the phone calls were for the older boys and we only had to buzz once for Donald or twice for

Bob. This method worked quite well. For supper, we would simply give a whole series of buzzes.

However, there were times when we called the ninth son, Steve, that meant nine buzzes and this confusion caused more than one to come downstairs, especially if it was near suppertime. When the supper call buzzes were heard, (nine plus) all the boys would come running down the back stairway. No one wanted to miss supper.

We also used a numbering system in the laundry room. Delores would average eight loads of laundry each day. She would put two loads in the two washers every morning before breakfast and when the washer buzzed at the finish, she would put these two loads in the two dryers and start two new loads in the washers. This would continue through out the day. As the washing came out of the dryer, it was folded and put on a large table according to the numbers. The children were responsible for picking up their laundry and putting it in dresser drawers and hangers. They were also responsible for the cleanliness of their rooms and sending soiled clothing down the center hall chute on the second floor to the basement. This was a very large chute with a large three feet square box in the basement laundry room to catch the clothes.

Someone once said, "you cannot teach a child to take care of himself unless you let him try to take care of himself." This we did. The children were required to pick up their laundry at the large table in the basement laundry room. Socks and clothes were initialed with white thread by Delores to identify the owners.

Sometimes, some piles of clean clothes would get bigger and bigger which meant the owner was not picking up their laundry. We would wonder what that person was wearing. We did not notice anyone wearing dirty clothes. It became obvious that some were using the laundry room table for storage instead of transferring the clean clothes to their dressers. They preferred to go to the basement and take what they needed to wear at any given time. This situation led to an announcement on the family large bulletin board that read *Pick up your laundry now number 7 and number 4 or else*. Delores never told me what the *or else* was, but I'm sure everyone else knew or at least they did not want to find out.

The ability to communicate an infraction of rules by number had the gracefulness to get the message across without being personal or demeaning. However, if this notice did not result in remedial action, the next step was to mention names after which there would be a one-on-one confrontation.

Friends would ask if there was any confusion with the numbers and there was some. Our children were not just numbers. But somehow this sequential system worked to solve many problems. With a little thought, they could identify anyone's number. Even Delores and I had to refer to our list occasionally to get the right number. The first number and the last number were easy but sometimes the others took a little effort. Did all the children feel comfortable knowing that they had a number? Yes, I believe so. They knew the number represented their position in the seniority sequence. They all knew that they were more than just a number. I think that they also appreciated the convenience the numbers gave them in solving some of our problems.

All the children even applied the numbers in a matter-of-fact manner both at home and in school. We were told by one of the children's teachers at school, during the parents—teacher's conferences, about an incident that happened shortly after little Mary Ann, one of our five-year-olds, started school. It seems that when Mary Ann started the first grade at St. Clare grade school, which was the same school that eight of her brothers and sisters were attending, her teacher, who was familiar with our family merger, asked her, "Well, so you're one of the Arsenault—McMillan family. And which one are you?"

"I'm number seventeen!" little Mary Ann McMillan happily replied.

Superstition

That single number *'seventeen'* kept re-occurring everywhere we turned. We are not superstitious but it was interesting to note how that certain numbers kept popping up over and over and sometimes in the most unusual places. I agree with the French philosopher and writer Jean Rousseau (1712-1778) who said, "I think we cannot too strongly attack superstition." But, I also agree with the English philosopher Francis Bacon (1561-1626) who said 150 years before Rousseau, "There is a superstition in avoiding superstition." So, it seems to me that taken in the light of these two great thinkers, that as long as superstition does not dominate decisions and life then these coincidences of events can be acceptable for what they are, an interesting and amusing comparisons of coincidental events.

It was in this light that we took note of the number seventeen and its frequency and repetitiveness of its appearance. I half-jokingly called this curiosity and coincidence to Delores' attention as the *writing on the wall*. I suggested that it was God's approval of our joint venture in marriage to raise these beautiful seventeen children. Be that what it may, we were always amazed to find another repetition of the number seventeen as we went about the business of raising this family.

It is interesting to note that the Bible has a whole book called *Numbers*. The Bible also speaks of the *seven days to build the world* if you count the *day of rest*. There were the *twelve* tribes of Israel and the *ten* lost tribes. The New Testament talks about the *twelve* apostles; the *three* persons in *one* God; Christ's *forty* days in the desert and the resurrection of Christ in *three* days. It goes on and on, and numbers with God seem to go together. We all would like God to give us a sign for direction. The Jews asked Moses for a sign from God when they doubted him. The *Ten Commandments* were written in stone by the *finger of God*. So, when the number seventeen kept appearing, it was easy for us to make some sort of evaluation and interpret this to be a sign from God that we were on the right track.

The seventeen miles of expressway from Allen Park to Grosse Pointe Park was the first occurrence. With some thought, I discovered that my phone number, 331-2710, added up to 17. Also, our car license numbers, BWK737 and LSX539, both added up to 17. The first apartment that I rented when I married Marge was 1707 Livernois in Detroit. My father's barbershop address was 717 Junction Avenue in Detroit. I'm not superstitious, but, as I often repeated to Delores, those number coincidences were so prevalent and frequent that I thought that if we had not gotten married and made a go of this merger, a bolt of lightning might have come down from heaven and struck both of us. It seemed to be our destiny.

On our first night after being married, the room at the Pontchartrain Hotel was 1017. It's nice to have everything working for you and it's nice to feel that God is on your side and helping you. *Nothing succeeds like success* when all your plans work out. I've discovered that it's not *Murphy's Law* that holds *if something can go wrong, it will and at the worse possible time.* No it's not Murphy's Law, it's the *devil*s. That sneaky devil is always trying to make life miserable for all and blaming it on somebody else. Even during World War II, the *gremlin* was another name for the devil and I remember the situation always was summed up as *snafu* (situation normal, all fouled up.) But, I think it was the devil that *fouled up* all the time. It's nice to think that God's on your side once in a while and he puts a stop to the sly diabolical antics of the devil.

XIII

Unity

Men's hearts ought not to be set against one another,
But set with one another, and all against evil only.
Thomas Carlyle 1795-1881

As I have stressed, family unity was one of our primary goals. So we were not only seeking *unity* for the strength derived from it, but unity in the love and understanding with compassion for one another as a family of brothers, sisters, and parents. We agreed that we needed *unity of command* as parents so that the children could not pit the father against the mother or vice versa. We did away with *ask your mother* or *ask your father* and *wait till I tell your father* or *wait till I tell your mother*. We agreed to make decisions together. As Abraham Lincoln stated in his speech at the Republican State Convention in Springfield, Illinois on July 17, 1858 (note the month and day is 717) "A house divided against itself cannot stand." He was quoting Christ from the Bible (Mark 3:25.) "…And if a house be divided against itself, that house cannot stand." So, we felt that one of our tasks would be to create an atmosphere of one united family

The family is an entity like a corporation that can succeed or lose together. For example, if the father gets a raise or promotion, then the family got a raise or promotion. It's not just one person. Also, if you want to be nice to me then be nice to my family. It works both ways. When you give something to a man who has a family, you're really giving something to the man *and* his family. This thesis also applies to the whole family. Be nice to each other and you're being nice to the parents. It's like Christ saying, "inasmuch as you did it for the least of my brethren, you did it for me." And so it goes. Luckily, our children always had a high regard for each other and many times they would come to the defense of each other. If I were to ask, "who broke the glass?" All were silent. No one snitched on the other. The children seemed to always be glad to help one another. I believe that they knew the value of unity and family. There is great comfort in knowing that you can always count on your brothers or sisters for help even if it's three o'clock in the morning and you're stuck somewhere on a lonely road. After all, if you can't depend on your own family, who can you depend on?

We were always trying to teach our children right from wrong. Many lessons of value were found on our large bulletin board from time to time. The following two verses, *If You'd Like To Have* and *The Men in the Ranks* were favorites that many of the children learned by heart and can repeat to this day. In the first verse, **home** can be changed to **church**, **family**, **teacher** or **anything**:

IF YOU'D LIKE TO HAVE
If you'd like to have the kind of a **home**;
Like the kind of a **home** you'd like.
You needn't pack your cloths in a bag,
And start on a long-long hike.
For you'll only find what you left behind,
For there's really nothing new;
It's a knock at yourself when you knock your home.
It isn't your **home** …it's you!

THE MEN IN THE RANKS
There are men in the ranks,
That will stay in the ranks.
Do you know why?
I'll tell you why.
Simply because they haven't;
The ability to get things done.

Here are samples of a few more of our bulletin board announcements and notices:

BE NICE
It's nice to be important,
But it's more important to be nice.

GET IT DONE
If you want something done,
Give it to a busy person.

And it will be done.

GET LUCKY
It's funny, but the harder you work;
The luckier you get.

GET TOUGH
When the going gets tough,
The tough get going.

Don't drink and drive.
Don't ride with anyone who drinks and drives.
Don't be a fool…Stay in school.
Birds of a feather flock together; so pick your own friends

Don't let them pick you.
If you want to know what kind of a person someone is,
Check out his friends.
Be careful who you chose for a friend.

In our capacity as parents we took the role of personnel managers. We did a lot of clipping from magazines and newspapers for the family bulletin board. When we saw something that we thought would be especially timely and pertinent to our family, up it went on the bulletin board. Some items were on the bulletin board only a few days. Others stayed up longer. For example, there was a plaque that stated:

A day is wasted without laughter.

Other Plaques

The best thing I ever have in my kitchen
is a friend that can cook. HELP WANTED.

Recipe for a happy kitchen;
A measure of good will,
A full cup of understanding;
Mix with joy,
And add plenty of love.

Bless this home and all who are in it.

True love is life's greatest treasure,
And it is a decision.

We also had some humorous signs that would occasionally find their way up on the family bulletin board.

Uncle Sam wants you!
Join the Navy and see the world.
Join the Peace Corps.
Become a priest.
Join a Nunnery.
Elope!
It's fun to run away.
Write if you find work.

I think that everyone of us has sometimes contemplated running away. We never really had any run-a-ways in our family except one. We would have been very hurt if anyone had really run away before the age of majority (whatever majority means.) Our children were just average among others but to us, as most parents, they were special. But, there was one incident when someone decided to run away. The story, as told by Delores, involves Marty when he was about five years old. Years before our marriage, Marty had decided that he had had enough.

"I'm going to run away," Marty emphatically told his mother.

"Oh, is that right? Do you want me to help you pack?"

"No!"

"Well, let me know when you're leaving."

"Okay."

So, Marty went to his room and returned with a little suitcase, stating, "I'm leaving now."

"Well, good-bye and write if you find work," his mother said.

Out the door went Marty. Unknown to Marty, one of the older brothers had been instructed by his mother to follow him and make sure that he didn't get lost or in trouble and that he didn't go too far. About ten minutes later, the front door bell rang. There was Marty with his suitcase.

"I want a ride," he demanded, "because I'm not allowed to cross the street."

"You get in here Marty!" his mother said. "It's almost supper time and I don't have the time to drive you. You'll just have to run away some other time."

Drugs & Alcohol

How did we deal with drugs and alcohol? That was a subject that we discussed frequently as a family. I would tell them "Don't be the one who gets drunk and have everybody laugh at you. When someone says to you 'man, I'm going to get drunk tonight,' he's really being ignorant. What he is really saying is 'I will dull my brain tonight, thus impairing my ability to see, hear, talk, walk, and think.' This is pretty dumb. He may as well say that he wants a brain tumor because the symptoms are the same. Once drunk, a person is vulnerable to attack and destruction by anyone sober since the ability to protect oneself is very noticeably impaired. A drunk becomes fair game for anyone who wants to take advantage of him. And, continued abuse of alcohol or drugs will deteriorate the body until finally your health degenerates into self destruction."

Drugs are just another form of self-abuse, except drugs are even more dangerous. These were some of the arguments that we used to warn our children about the use of drugs and alcohol. We tried to teach our children that they should avoid drugs like poison. Only at the prescribed direction of a doctor for the cure of illnesses should drugs be taken. It is ignorant to gamble on drugs for pleasure.

We also tried to teach moderation in all things. Excesses in anything and nature usually makes you pay a price. Even in over-eating, there's obesity that can lead to many illnesses and disabling diseases with an early death. Moderation is the key word for a healthy and, hopefully, a long life

Questions

When hearing that we had a large family, many friends would ask us, "How do you keep track of them?" Well, it wasn't easy. But, Delores developed a sixth sense about it. She could almost feel when someone was missing or not where he or she was supposed to be. Delores became very acute to sensing who was not in at night. She said that she never was able to sleep until everyone was in the house. Mothers are endowed with a special instinct to watch over their children. And the mother of seventeen had developed this instinct to a high degree of awareness and perception for the welfare of her children. This was all part of our good management and control.

We had a rule. Whenever anyone was out in the evenings, with permission of course, they were required to knock on our bedroom door when they got in if it was after we had gone to bed. It's not that we wanted to be awakened. It's just that we cared about them. If we did not care, we would never ask any questions and there would not be any rules. They could run wild. But, we did care and we do care…very much so. That's why we had an *in and out* sheet on the family bulletin board. They were expected to sign *in and out* whenever they went somewhere other than school. There was a column for when they were expected back and where they went. This worked pretty well. The children were good about leaving this information. It also helped to be able to tell their friends when they would be home for callbacks.

Our teenagers were concerned with communicating and going out with their friends. However, sometimes they would have to answer certain questions about their comings and goings. When the teenagers who had driver's licenses would ask to borrow the car, they would have to answer some pertinent questions for this privilege of borrowing the car. The questions were as follows:

> Where are you going?
> With whom are you going?
> How long will you be gone?
> When will you return?
> Is your homework done?
> Is your room clean?

If they were able to satisfactorily answer these questions, permission and the car keys would be granted, but they were still required to sign out.

At times I felt that a rule of knocking on our bedroom door was carried a bit too far. In the middle of the night there would be a knock on our bedroom door waking me up. Delores would be awake waiting for that knock. One night I was awakened from my sleep by a knock on our bedroom door.

"Who's there?" Delores asked in a whisper.

"It's me. I'm home! Did I get any phone calls?" Someone whispered back.

"No. Good night and go to bed." Delores would answer in a tired manner looking at the clock to check the time.

"OK. Good night."

Then I would turn over and think to myself, "who was that? I bet it was Tim. I think he was the only one that was still out and would want to chitchat at this ungodly hour.

The next morning, I would interrogate Delores.

"Was it Tim that knocked on our door when he came in last night."

"Yes. We talked for quite a while."

"What time was it?"

"It was late."

A little later, Tim came down and sat at the breakfast table.

"What time did you knock on our door last night?" his mother would ask.

"I don't know," Tim answered, "but it was early."

"Early in the morning?"

"No, it wasn't. I remember that it was just around eleven thirty. And, by the way, can't I have my own house key?"

"No! We've got enough keys around here. Just remember to put it back on the key rack for someone else."

Notice the strategy and tactic used by Tim. When after collecting data, it was determined that no one knew for certain what time he came in, then, it was as always *around eleven o'clock,* the curfew hour for sixteen year olds. *Around* was a matter of interpretation. The next step was to quickly change the subject. "Why can't I have my own house key?" was a diversion tactic. There's no doubt. We had a lot of smart children.

Who gets their own key to the house? Everyone wants his or her own key. But, we decided that they would get their own key at the age of seventeen. Otherwise, they would have to use the spare key on the key rack. The *key* was a clear indication of our trust in their maturity and when given to someone, it meant that we were confident of their good sense of responsibility and trust. This thinking goes with the adage: *Give someone a good reputation and there's a good chance they will live up to it and not let you down.* It was just another lesson to learn when growing up in a large family.

Training

There are many lessons to be learned while growing up as a member of a large family and the opportunity for family unity and concern were not the only lessons. A large family gives everyone the chance to learn the art of getting along with others. How to win friends and get along with people can easily be learned from the ins and out of daily living. Everyone was a different unique person with his or her own personalities. The task of everyone striving to understand and appreciate each other with each one's special talents was an everyday encounter. It was a matter of learning to give and take in appreciation and understanding that was learned by osmosis.

Delores often said, "A large family at home is the perfect training ground for human relations and personnel management. If a person can learn the lessons of living in a large family, then living with the outside world becomes a piece of cake." It was our premise that happiness is not measured by *how much you can do for yourself*, but by *how much you can do for others*. The training and opportunity for *doing something for somebody else* starts right in the home from the crib on up. Delores, who earned a bachelor's degree from Marygrove University, with a major in Early Education, knew that the training and love starts at birth and the first few years of a child are the most important for any child.

Delores had always wanted a large family and she felt that she could do a good job. She felt a large family was a great gift to give to her children as long as one could afford them. The advantage of many brothers and sisters added strength to each one. One can always turn to your brother or sister for help when needed. Growing up with a large family is not only a learning process for the children but also for the parents. It is interesting to observe that when parents finally get good at their job as parents and the children get good at their jobs as children it's all over and the time comes for the children in the family to leave and make their own way in this life. Thus, the cycle goes on as God has decreed, *a time for everything*. It is hoped that when the children leave, they will be better parents than we because they had the advantage of growing up in a large family. Many do not have that unique advantage when they were young.

XIV

Money

The use of money is all the advantage there is in having it.
Ben Franklin 1706-1790

Money and budget management are a very important part of our family planning and we included money management in our family teaching endeavor to our children. We wanted to initiate the children in what we thought was the correct and pragmatic approach to money. There are many axioms about money, all good and important to remember. For starters, Benjamin Franklin, (who became one of the most successful and wealthiest men in America) owned 18 paper mills, invented daylight saving time, discovered the Gulf Stream, invented the stove named after himself, bifocals, electric explosives, and the public libraries. He left us with a wealth of axioms about money, e.g.: *A penny saved is a penny earned; It's hard for an empty bag to stand upright. Most problems are money problems.*

My own mother, who called herself *just a farm girl* said, "it's not how much money you earn that makes the difference, it's how much money you save." She opened bank accounts for my brother and sister in our names when we were still young children.

Time is money it has been said. We spend 35 to 40 years of eight-hour days working for money. But, there are some things more important than money. Take *health* for example. Money without health is worthless. If our health fails, we would gladly spend our money to regain our health if we could. That's why we should plan for those golden retirement years when we will no longer have to trade our time to work for money. Careful money management and healthy habits in youth will allow us to have the time for our money later on. Benjamin Franklin said that during our working years, *most problems are money problems*, but, Ben Franklin had enough money to retire at the age of 42 and that's when he stopped working for money. He turned over all his business to his partner, David Hall, and for the next 42 years, he had the time and money to pursue all of his many interests in astronomy, politics, and inventions without worrying about money. He died at the age of 84, still a rich man. These were some of the thoughts and axioms that we tried to instill in our children.

Years ago, during the Great Depression of the late twenties and early thirties, everyone seemed to be out of work and looking for a job. The expression *write if you find work* became an expression used for people leaving their home looking for work. The search went to other cities and other states. People would go wherever there was work. Some even went to Alaska looking for gold. An older friend of mine went to Alaska looking for gold in 1933. He didn't find gold, but he did find work…fishing. He said he found *the gold in salmon fish*ing.

These values and truism we tried to pass on to our seventeen children. As children, we go to school to learn the things that will help us find work. The better and more we learn, the better job we can get and the more money we will be able to make. That's part of life in the big city. We work to take care of our families and ourselves.

I have always felt that the value of a person was in the ability to work. It was not how much money he has, but it was in what a person was capable of doing. What value is money or good looks if you're lost on a desert island? The ability to do things and get things done increases the value of a person. A person is only worth what he can do for himself and for his friends. I believe that the ability to get constructive things done and to make a contribution to society is their own ultimate reward for hard work. I believe that we need to work just for our own mental health. Benjamin Franklin said, "An idle mind is the devil's workshop."

These were some of the thoughts and the philosophy that became part of our family philosophy. Old Ben Franklin once wrote, *"If you know how to spend less than you make, you have the philosopher's stone."* We wanted to teach our children the habit of saving. And it is a habit. I would tell them to *always save ten percent of what you make. Pay yourself first*. Their grandfather, A. Z. Shmina, would give the children a five-dollar bill and tell them not to spend it. "Keep it for an emergency," he would say. He knew the value of money. He came to this country at the age of fifteen from Romania, which was part of the Ottoman Empire, with only five gold pieces that his father gave him. He worked in a restaurant washing dishes at night to get his degree as an engineer. He retired as chairman of the board of A. Z. Shmina & Sons Construction Company…competing with Darin & Armstrong, Barton Mallow and other large construction companies.

So, from the very beginning, when the children would receive money for their birthdays or other reasons, Delores and I would tell them, "put it in the bank." From the very start of our *joint venture,* one of the first things that we did was to open bank accounts at the NBD Bank for each of the seventeen children. The older boys had paper routes and the older girls did baby sitting. The habit of saving was started at a very early age. Many of the children ended up with sizable amounts of money in their accounts, which helped them later during their college years. For example, Donald McMillan, our oldest, having won a scholastic scholarship to the University of Detroit, used his bank savings to buy his first used car, a Ford T Bird, and to pay for one summer of studies at Oxford University in England.

Delores would do all the banking and weekly she would take the seventeen bankbooks to deposit a dollar here and two dollars there into the individual accounts. The tellers at the bank would always ask the usual questions when they saw all the bankbooks:

"How do you manage such a large family?"
"Who does all the cooking?"
"Who does all the washing?"
"Who does all the cleaning?"
"How do you keep track of seventeen children?"
"I'll bet you could write a book."

Budgeting

All needs regarding expenditures for the household were always a joint decision. All major expenditures were carefully analyzed and studied. "Get three bids," I would always say. That was one basic requirement at GM for all project expenditures. I worked in property records and was knowledgeable of capital expenditures. In our joint-decision making, we took the same approach. We had the added advantage of our own expertise to contribute to the decisions. Delores was an expert homemaker and manager. I would do the bookkeeping and analysis. Incidentally, in the event of a bad decision, we would share the blame. No one person was at fault.

The study of budgeting, as I have said, played a very important role in our final decision to attempt this marriage. Uniting two large families as we did could never have succeeded without careful planning and management. We knew that. I had made several budget plans for our anticipated expenditures months before we were married just to convince ourselves that we could do it.

Our budgeting was based on the following thesis: It is important to think of a budget as a changing and dynamic planning document. It should always remain flexible and the ability to adjust budgets to current needs and events is very important. Budgeting can be viewed as a road map used to achieve planned objectives or goals. First, we set goals and objectives, and then decisions are made as to what priorities are used to get to goal. Sometimes there were many roads that could be taken. Style of living, income, fixed costs and variable costs would dictate the necessary decisions that must be made to attain budget goal objectives.

Budgeting is similar to the navigational art of *dead reckoning* that a sailor uses to set course and direction. It is based on all known factors that would affect the course and direction, such as wind direction, current speed, water depth, and compass readings. The *dead reckoning* course is adjusted and re-plotted from time to time as new data and information are collected. So is the planned budget. The budget was always adjusted as we made new decisions regarding priorities and needs.

Here are a few axioms that helped us make decisions as to our needs and necessities on our budget:

Whatever you can't afford is expensive at any price.
Save ten percent for yourself even if you have to borrow money.
A bad or incomplete budget plan is better than no plan at all.
Budgets are dynamic and change is inevitable.

Money Managers

People would sometimes ask, "How can you afford to send all your seventeen children to college?" The answer was, "We can't totally." But, in our family, anyone who wanted to go to college went to college. However, if we were to pay for the college education of seventeen children, we had to consider the high cost when the *multiple progression phenomenons* take effect. For example, if college tuition were two thousand dollars a month, we'd have to spend $34,000 for one year's college education. "Who gets what and how much," was a money management decision that we had to contend with every day. We have been guided by the thesis that *God helps those who help themselves.* We decided we would pay the initial costs for the first semester for anyone. If they chose a college near home, that would help reduce college expenses. They would get whatever Social Security allotted for them while they stayed in college. The McMillans also were eligible for a small amount that the Veterans Administration would pay if the children stayed in college up to the age of 21. They could get part time jobs and, when needed, we would give them some money to stay in college.

The children's grandfather, A. Z. Shmina, also gave them some money to help pay college expenses. The children were ambitious and worked not only part time jobs, but summer jobs. I was able to get some of them summer jobs at the Fisher Body Fleetwood Plant where I worked. These would be temporary jobs during the summer model-change-over but they would get the wages that General Motors paid all production workers. All in all, somehow the children all learned to manage their money and were able to stay in college and work their way through. Also, our children discovered there are government loans, grants, and other financial aids available. So, *Budgeting* and *Money Management* were two of the all important lessons that we tried to teach our children while growing up in the *big house* with the *big family* in the *big city.*

XV

Automobiles

The sum of the whole is this: Walk and be happy.
Walk and be healthy.
The best way to lengthen out our days is to walk steadily
and with a purpose.
Charles Dickens 1812-1870

"The board meeting will come to order!" I said as we sat around the dinner table.

"Now, what is this problem about cars?"

"Well, I need the car to go to the football game," sixteen-year-old Tim, said.

"But I need it to go to the library," big Mary Ann said.

"What about me?" sixteen-year-old Patrick asked. "I need the car too."

"We can't afford cars for every driver," Delores said. "With the high school five miles away that's why we have a car pool. We have to share my car since Dad needs his car to go to work so that's not available."

"What we need is a special car for the children," I suggested. "Maybe this family needs three cars instead of two...one for me to go to work, one for mother to do the shopping and run errands, and one for the children to share for a school car pool, the library, shopping, part time work, dates, and all the other reasons they have for borrowing their parents cars."

"Yea, that's what we need. Our own car," everyone chorused.

"It would be cheaper to insure a third small car for the children's exclusive use than to have them all listed and insured on our bigger cars," I said. "That way we could insure the large cars exclusively for the parents…one for work and one for pleasure."

Cars were a problem, as well as they were costly and they can be dangerous. A few years after we first were married, we had four teenage drivers and two family cars. After a few minor accidents, some speeding tickets, and the demand to borrow our cars, we knew we had a car problem. What would we do when we knew we had thirteen more teenage drivers? What was the best way to solve the dilemma? The transportation needed serious and careful analysis to resolve it satisfactorily. Rule one of scientific decision making was to identify the problem. We had too many teenage drivers for only two cars. That was the problem. What's more, new drivers seemed to have frequent fender benders, speeding tickets and other infractions of the traffic laws. All these problems were brought to the dinner board meeting.

The questions I asked were always the same:

"Why did you get a speeding ticket and how can this be avoided?"

"What can we do to protect ourselves against these problems?"

The discussions helped everyone understand the problems that new drivers face. All learned a lot. Even those who were not yet drivers learned from these deliberations and discussions.

We had two large station wagons that the teenage drivers had to borrow when they needed a car. Both were relatively new. Both had high-powered V8 engines. One of our drivers with four of his friends in the car got a ticket speeding eighty five miles an hour on a sixty-five-mile-an-hour expressway. How do we prevent this from happening again? That was the problem that led to a children's car.

The Opel

Delores and I decided that a smaller car was needed for the young drivers…a car with less horsepower, a car that would not be allowed on the expressway by our orders, a car that would not be used for *joy riding, a* car that would be used only for trips to the library, school and for work. We found a good used four-cylinder four-door Opel station wagon. Our insurance costs went down when we took the teenage drivers off the big car and insured them only on the Opel, with no collision. The Opel had only liability insurance.

The tickets and fender benders stopped even as four more teenage drivers joined the teenage family drivers. It was a stick shift; so all had to learn to drive a stick shift. All went well until a car ran a stop street and drove into the side of our Opel, broad siding the wagon just hard enough to turn it over on its side. Luckily, the four girls in the car escaped injury because they were wearing their seat belts and neither car was going fast. Our teenage daughter, Ann Louise, the driver, and her three friends were on their way to the library when the accident occurred. The other driver's insurance company totaled the Opel and they paid us the salvage value of seven hundred dollars.

We kept the money as well as the car. We fixed the broken side windows with Plexiglas and bumped out the fenders. We hand painted the dents. So what are a few dents? With only these repairs, it was still good, cheap and dependable transportation. We were getting close to thirty miles to the gallon.

There were rules for use of this car, which included approval from the parents at all times. Sightseeing drives and touring were not allowed and drives on the expressways were definitely out. No one wanted to drive it faster then the thirty-five-mile-per-hour speed limit anyway because of the rattles in the car. Actually these rules were easy to follow because the way the car looked, rattled and shook, it was no pleasure when it went faster than twenty-five miles per hour. A new rule went up on the family bulletin board after the accident; *Wear your seat belts to remind you to drive safely.*

The whole episode turned out to be beneficial. The Opel looked like a wreck. But it solved our problems of teenage drivers and slowed them down. One look at the Opel and everyone was reminded to wear seat belts and drive safely. It was a stick shift and everyone had to learn to shift gears. The green Opel became a legend in its own time. It was seen all around the Grosse Pointes. It was seen at many high school homecoming parades with all kinds of water paints decorating the many dents. One of our daughters, Margaret Elizabeth, wrote an endearing poem about the Opel.

OUR DEAR OPEL CAR

Oh Opel car, how sad you look.
One side of you is all smashed.
Your passenger door doesn't open any more,
And you haven't been the same
Since you crashed.

You're only three,
To the world, you look ten.
To me, you look even older.
But, Opel dear, at heart you're young
Though physically,
You just get moldier.
In the winter I freeze,
In the summer I bake.
Though these hardships,
I hardly consider.

It's my friends who gripe.
Make unkind jokes and laugh,
When you cough and sputter.

So, Opel dear, take heart…don't fret;
You know we'll never desert you.
So long as your engine
Continues to gurgle,
Your brakes never fail,
When we need you.

XVI

Diversions

The mind ought sometime to be diverted, that it may return the better to thinking.
Phaedrus 14-54 AD

Summer vacations were another consideration in our family planning sessions. Everyone wanted the family to take a vacation together. With nineteen persons in a family, where can they all go together and still keep the costs reasonable? Cruises and flying would be too expensive. How far can we go? A day's drive would be the best we could expect. That meant someplace within four or five hundred miles. Since my work only allowed two weeks vacation, that would be the duration of our trip. Will everybody be going? Everybody up to the oldest wanted to go.

These were some of the questions that were posed at the dinner table board meetings. After all, if other families went on vacation, why can't and shouldn't we? Being a big family was not a good reason to be different from any other family when it comes to vacations. A discussion was held at the dinner table with many suggestions:

"All those who want to go on a vacation somewhere this summer say aye," I said.

"Aye!" everyone answered.

"The *ayes* have it."

"Question: where do we want to go? The ocean, mountains, seashore, the Great Lakes or Alaska?"

"Alaska!" they all shouted.

"Just kidding. You'll have to go to Alaska on your own. I think we should stick to the Great Lakes. Michigan is a beautiful place for summer vacations."

"Let's just go somewhere," Delores said.

"I think a trip up north would be the most practical. What we need is a cottage that will sleep nineteen people."

"Where will we ever find such a cottage?" Joe asked.

"We'll have to start looking in the papers for cottages for rent and make some inquiries."

"I'll check the Grosse Pointe News for listings," Tish volunteered.

"Let's try to go to Burt Lake or somewhere on Lake Huron," I suggested.

"When we get some phone numbers, we can call the people and find out how many their cottages will accommodate. Maybe they can give us some suggestions," 'Big' Mary Ann said.

"Many times, cottages have a screened in porch with a few cots to accommodate more people," Mark added.

"And maybe we'll need two cottages," Delores said.

"They would need to be close to each other to be of any fun."

"I bet we could borrow a large tent from the Boy Scouts and we could go camping," Steve remarked.

"Sorry. Tents are not for me," Delores said. "I want hot and cold running water and a chrome-plated bathroom."

"This is our first vacation as a family of nineteen, and I don't think that a tent is the right answer," I said. We're going to be roughing it up enough as it is. Nice suggestion anyway, Steve."

"I think that a week up North at a Michigan Lake with two cottages next to each other would be great," Doc suggested.

It was agreed that we would search the papers for a couple of cottages up North and we would plan for a week on one of Michigan's lakes.

Everyone was enthusiastic about the vacation and all wanted to go. Everyone started watching the papers for rental cottages. A day's drive would get us as far as the Mackinac Bridge. Our target would be somewhere near Topinabee at Burt Lake or Alpena on Lake Huron somewhere in Michigan.

We found a cottage at Burt Lake that had six bedrooms. It was really two cottages that had been connected together making one large family room and kitchen. There was a fireplace and plenty of wood in the woodpile. The rent was only two hundred dollars for a week. The owner said that he normally did not rent it except for a few weeks in the summer to help pay for upkeep. We decided to rent it for one week with the intention of adding a second week if all went well and we liked it.

"Where on Burt Lake?" Patrick asked when the news was announced at the dinner table.

"I looked it up," Doc said. "It's near Indian River where there's a shrine with the world's biggest crucifix. The statue of Christ is suppose to weigh seven tons and the cross made of redwood is fifty five feet high and weighs fourteen tons."

"We can go to Mass there," Margaret suggested.

"It's almost to the Mackinac Bridge," I said. "And maybe we can make a side trip to see the bridge."

"Where's the bridge," Marty asked.

"It's about three hundred miles from here straight north," I said. "It connects the Lower Peninsula to the Upper Peninsula at St. Ignace. The bridge is five miles long and it is alleged to be the longest suspension bridge in the world."

"Boy, I'd sure like to see that," Robert said.

"Well, we can all see the bridge and some of the Upper Peninsula when we make a day trip from our home base at Burt Lake," I suggested.

"You mean we can cross the five-mile bridge?" Sue asked.

"Yes, it's just a short drive from Burt Lake. We can visit St. Ignace, one of the oldest cities in Michigan," I added. "It's where the founder Father Marquette is buried."

"There's a statue of Father Marquette at the entrance to Belle Isle right here in Detroit," Doc said.

Vacations

The planning for our first family northern vacation continued. We knew the destination and the cost. We were busy planning what kind of luggage we would need to transport nineteen people to the two cottages.

"None of the children except Doc and Bob has any luggage," Delores said.

"Now, that's a problem. Maybe we can use cardboard boxes."

"That's a good idea," everyone chimed in.

"But, they have to be the right size. Not too big and not too small. We will not have room for big boxes. We can use roof racks on the two station wagons, but how many boxes can we tie on each rack?"

"I've got an idea," Tim said. "We can go to Lou's Party Store on Charlevoix and see what kind of boxes he has."

Beer Cases

The next day at the dinner table, Tim reported that Lou suggested that we use empty beer cases. He said that he would loan us seventeen empty beer cases for our trip and we can bring them back when we return. They were clean and just the right size and would be easy to tie them to the racks. Everyone would have an empty beer case for his or her clothes.

"That's a great idea," I said. "Why didn't I think of that? They're the right size and shape and sturdy enough for the trip. They'll be easy to tie to the racks. Can you imagine seventeen beer cases on the roof of our two station wagons? What a sight."

"I wonder what our neighbors are going to say when they see us leaving with all those beer cases," Delores said.

"I can hear them now," Doc said. "There goes Delores and George. I guess their family really like beer."

"What the neighbors say is the least of our problems," I said. "Besides, I'm sure the grapevine will keep every neighbor informed with the correct information."

Driving North

Early in the morning of the day of departure, two station wagons left 1000 Devonshire heading for the Michigan North Country. Delores and I had our station wagons loaded with luggage and children. Delores had all the eight girls and Doc, our seventeen-year-old boy, who would help her drive. I had the remaining eight boys in my station wagon. Seventeen beer cartons were neatly stacked on the top luggage carriers of both cars.

Everyone had their own box with their name stuck on the top. All those beer cases on top of two cars were a sight to see.

We had driven for about three hours and I wondered why Delores seemed to have a problem keeping up. I kept slowing down to let her catch up with us. Finally, I signaled for her to follow me at the next rest stop area. When we stopped, I told Delores that she was driving too slowly.

"Delores, "you're not keeping up with me. You're only going about forty miles an hour. Can't you go any faster? We should be doing the speed limit of fifty five mile per hour if we ever want to get there."

"I'm sorry," she said. "I'm going as fast as the car will go. I've got my foot all the way down on the gas pedal."

"Well, OK," I said. "But, look why don't you let Doc take the wheel until the next rest stop. We still have another four hours of driving ahead of us."

"Good idea," she said as she went around to the passenger side of the car.

"Sure. I'll be glad to drive," Doc said.

"You and your mother take turns driving," I said. "Every couple of hours at a rest stop area you can change off."

As I pulled out of the rest stop area and merged into the traffic, I began to accelerate up to fifty mile per hour. I kept my eye on Delores' station wagon with Doc driving to see if they could keep up with me. Looking into the rearview mirror, I saw Doc right behind me. Whatever was wrong with the car seems to be all right now, I thought. Doc was right behind me when we pulled up to a stop at the next rest stop area.

"The car must have fixed itself," I said as I approach Delores' car.

"Yes. It works fine," Doc said. I had no trouble keeping up with you. I could have even gone faster if I wanted to."

"I don't know what the matter was," Delores said.

"Doc, how tall are you?" I asked.

"Oh, about five ten, I guess. Why?"

"And, Delores," I said ignoring his question for the moment. "How tall are you?"

"About five two."

"Did either of you change the seat positions?"

"No."

"Delores, you're eight inches shorter than Doc. Do you think that maybe your foot was not reaching the floorboard? You were extending your foot all the way but it may not have been to the floorboard. When you pushed all the way down on the gas pedal, you may not have been far enough down so forty-five miles per hour was all you could reach. This time when you take over from Doc, move the seat forward so that you're sure that you can reach the floorboard and I'll bet your car will go faster."

"Well, I'll be," Delores, said. "By George, I think you've got it. I purposely did not move the seat forward when I started driving because I knew Doc would be driving and he needs more legroom with his long legs. I think you've solved the problem, George. Let's see if I can keep up with you now."

That was the end to the slow-car problem. Delores moved the seat forward and from then on, she had no problem keeping up.

Burt Lake

The cottage was just as promised. Six bedrooms would accommodate all the girls, the boys, Delores and me very nicely. A beautiful beach was right in front of the cottage. The water was beautiful. You could walk out quite a way before you got to five feet of water. This was great for the children. The evenings were cool, so we made a fire in the fireplace every evening.

After a few days, the owners came by the cottage with a saddled pony.

"We thought the children would enjoy a pony ride," they said.

"They sure would," I agreed. "Most of them have never been on a real live pony."

"Great, horseback riding," Bob, said. "I'll get the movie camera. We've got to have this on film."

"Good idea," I said. "Everyone can take a turn riding the pony and we'll take pictures of each one of you just like the old western round up of cowboys and cowgirls riding on the range."

Everyone rode the pony, including me. Tim and Joe were able to gallop a little way but when I tried riding the pony, he must have thought that I was too heavy and the pony tried to scrape me off by rubbing me up against a tree. Smart pony!

All in all, all had a fun time and the pony ride was great for the children.

"I hear that you all went to see the Mackinac Straits Bridge," the owner's wife said. "How did you like the trip?" speaking to Janet Arsenault, one of our four-year olds.

"Fine, thank you," Janet answered.

"And you," pointing to four-year-old little Mary Ann McMillan, "what did you see on your trip?"

"We saw where one of daddy's friends is buried," she answered.

We all laughed. "She's referring to the Father Marquette's National Memorial grave site at St. Ignace," I said. "I guessed she thought that Father Marquette was a friend of mine because of all the fuss I made about his burial site."

Poison Ivy

"Dad, I've got an itch and a rash all over my legs," Bob said to me showing me his red skinned legs.

"Were you walking bare legged in the weeds?"

"Well, there's a bunch of weeds around where I pulled the boat up from the beach."

"It looks like a case of poison ivy. Tell everyone to stay out of the weeds. Pass the word around. Meanwhile, see your mother and have her put some lotion on it. Try not to scratch it."

Outside of poison ivy and a few other minor problems, everyone in the family had a great time swimming, fishing and touring on our first vacation as a family. We would have extended it another week, but the owners said that they were expecting some of their family and they would not be able to rent us another week. I secretly think that although the owners liked having us there, the septic tanks would not take another week of nineteen people flushing the two toilets. We had been told by the owner not to flush all the time. I never realized that septic tanks could fill up and overflow.

The summer vacation up north was great fun and all agreed that we should do it again the following year. All went well on our drive back to 1000 Devonshire and we all arrived safe and sound with our seventeen beer cases on top of the cars and none the worse after being away only one week. *Be it ever so humble, there's no place like home.*

Lake Huron

The following summer, we made plans to rent the same Burt Lake cottage again. But, it was not available. However, we were able to rent a cottage right on Lake Huron a few miles south of Alpena where the water temperature in July never gets any warmer than sixty degrees.

Not many wanted to go swimming that year. We felt that it was important for all to go swimming at least once on every summer vacation. So, that summer was born the new *Polar Bear Club*. All were invited to be members. The initiation consisted of swimming in the beautiful Lake Huron waters. Preparation included taking 8mm movies of the event. The initiation ceremonies for the inductees would be a joint swim for all the new *Polar Bears* as they were made members of this exclusive club. Delores was ready with the movie camera to properly record the great event. We were all lined up on the beach and when I counted to three, we would all run into the water and dive in headfirst. All, including me, agreed to this method of initiation. As we all ran into the water we were to shout *Polar Bear* as we all dived in headfirst.

The theory and hypothesized was: the body heat would last for several minutes and if you could jump in and out right away, you wouldn't feel the cold and you would become an honored member of the *Polar Bears*.
Simple. All were ready when the count went to *one, two, three go*! All in the line went running for the water as a long line of runners. All dove into the water except one…Patrick. As we looked back, Patrick, one of our twelve year olds, had, at the last minute, stopped short and was standing high and dry on the beach laughing. There was an immediate agreement by all that Patrick would join the *Polar Bears* and become a member in good standing. Needless to say, as a large group of brothers and sisters turned to assist Patrick, he jumped into the water and diving head first, he

became a member of the great *Polar Bear Club*. He was duly given membership into this select and elite group.

Our family vacation was wonderful and all the way home, we sang, *Hail, Hail, The Gangs All Here, Freckles Was His Name*, and *There's A Hole In The Bottom Of The Sea*.

XVII

Holidays

The luxury of doing for others surpasses every other personal enjoyment.
John Gay 1685-1732.

"What costume can I wear for Halloween?" was a question coming from each of the children as the last day of October came around.

"Use your imagination and dress up as something, " Delores said.

"That's right. The best costumes are right from your imagination," I said in agreement.

That settled the issue. The children and Delores created costumes and disguises for Halloween. Delores had designed and made a costume of a rabbit for the previous Easter. This rabbit costume was one that was ready for use when Halloween came around. This was the time of year when strange characters would suddenly take form. It was a challenge for all the children to make their own costumes. The rabbit costume was especially successful and appeared year after year with different people in it. Delores was the first to appear as the rabbit. Later, anybody who was near five feet tall would take over the costume.

After Halloween, came Thanksgiving, another memorable time. The entire family would participate in the Thanksgiving Day decorations in preparation of the big family turkey dinner. Delores' father and mother, grandparents, and my mother would attend with some of uncles and aunts. They would all bring something for the dinner. It was nothing to seat thirty-five or forty for dinner with all the trimmings. Usually we had two turkeys and a large ham buffet style. I would carve the two turkeys and I would also slice the ham with my super butcher type meat-slicer.

Before Thanksgiving could cool down, we were busy making plans for Christmas. This was the most anticipated holiday of all. It would start with the family going to a tree farm to look for the *right* Christmas tree. We needed one about eighteen-feet for the center hall entrance because the main staircase would go up about ten steps to a large landing that would turn for about six feet and then continue up another five steps. There was a large hammered brass center chandelier hanging from the ceiling of the second floor down to just above the first floor. This area was perfect for the Christmas tree.

At the tree farm, we would look for the biggest tree and it had to be a thin tree so as to not be too heavy. But we needed a full tree that would look nice.

"That tree is too small," big Mary Ann said as we looked at a Scotch pine in the grove.

"Here's one that's really big," Robert shouted from across the way.

Everyone ran over to check out Robert's big tree. All agreed that this tree would reach up to the second floor of our stairway hall entrance. The tree farmer said that it would cost five dollars a foot and the tree we had picked was about seventeen feet.

"There's that number again!" Marty said.

"We'll take it," I said, "if we can tie it up to the rack on my station wagon.

"Sure. We'll help you," he said.

"If a little is good, bigger is better," Tim said.

"Are you sure it's safe to carry this home?" Delores asked.

"Leave that to me," I said. "We have fifty feet of rope to tie it up with and we have plenty of able bodied man power to help put it on the roof and take it off. We'll just take our time going home and stay off the expressway.

"Well, George, I hope you know what you're doing," Delores said.

"Trust me," I said as I went around to start cutting the tree down.

"We'll hold it up," Joe said as he held on to some branches.

"No. Stand back everyone and let the tree fall in the clearing to the right."

I went to the right and cut a V-shaped notch. Then I went behind the notch and began to cut towards the notch.

"Here she comes!" Patrick shouted.

"Timber!" I yelled, just for the effect, as the tree slowly bent over and fell to the ground right where we wanted it to fall. All available hands picked it up and we carried it over to the car and placed it on the top roof rack. The tree extended a little over the hood of the car and over the trunk. We tied a red flag on it for safety. The trip back home was a happy ride, which included a stop at McDonald's for hot chocolate and hamburgers. It was the usual order of seventeen hamburgers and seventeen hot chocolates. The clerk, who took the order, asked me to repeat it twice more. Then she called her manager who filled the order.

Our first Christmas tree in the new house was perfect. It reached up to the second floor in the entrance hallway staircase. With the new tree stand, it reached up about eighteen feet. Getting the tree through the front door was a task that took a little patience. "Easy does it," I said as the boys and I carried it through the large oak door.

The decorations started a little at a time. Everyone did his or her part. We would walk up the stairway and hang decorations and lights reaching over the banister all the way up to the second floor. The older boys used a ladder to decorate the other side. By the end of the week the tree was mostly decorated. There was always something that someone wanted to add to the tree. But, when all the lights were up and turned on, it lit up the downstairs and the second floor hallway. Tall Christmas trees became the tradition for the front hall stairway. It was the focal point for all the festivities of a joyful season that lasted the month of December. Presents for the grandparents and a few others were placed under the tree and added color to the decorations. But, the best presents, the ones from *Santa Claus,* would be hidden and never be seen until Christmas morning. The Christmas tree decorating effort was never really complete until the nineteen Christmas stockings were hung on the banister all the way up the front staircase. Delores made sure that everyone had a Christmas stocking with his or her name on it

"When is Santa Claus coming?" little Mary Ann asked.

"On Christmas Eve when everyone is sleeping." Delores said.

"I don't believe that," Marty said.

"Only those who believe, receive."

"Oh, I believe," Mary, said. "I really believe." And a whole chorus of "I believe" went up from everybody.

"So do I," Delores said.

"We'll all go to Midnight Mass and after Mass, we can have a light snack and off to bed so Santa Claus can come with the presents," I said thinking of the job ahead for Delores and me.

"Whoever wakes up first, wake me up," Marty said not wishing to miss out on Christmas morning.

"Me too," a chorus replied.

Christmas

How do the parents of seventeen children decide who gets what and how much? Delores devised a method to do just that in an equitable manner. She put a Santa Claus list of all the names on the family bulletin board and it was up to the children to place their orders to Santa Claus. The necessary sizes and colors would also be noted. Santa Claus had said that he would try to get at least two of the items for everybody. The Santa Clause list went up when the Christmas tree went up. So, there was always plenty of time for the children to make up their minds. Santa was especially good at filling orders for clothes. But, a few toys and games were among the many items from Santa. There was a toy room in the basement reserved for all the games and toys accumulated from seventeen children. Each Christmas would add to our collection.

Delores and I decided that the recreation room in the basement would be the room where Santa Claus would leave the presents on Christmas morning. It was a ballroom with hardwood flooring and a fireplace. This would spare the upstairs and make it easier to keep neat. The basement recreation room was a very nice room. As I had mentioned before, there was a small 'bar room' attached to the recreation room with a lock on the door. This room was always locked before Christmas because that was where Santa Claus would store all the presents until Christmas morning.

At 5 a.m., Christmas morning, Delores and I had finally finished setting up all the presents. We had been up all night, having gone to Midnight Mass and then working to get everything ready after the last one went to bed. This was the children's first Christmas in the new house.

"We might as well stay up now," I said to Delores as we put the finishing touches on our work.

"It's all right with me. We can catch some sleep later."

"Maybe," I said. As I set up the movie camera on tri-pods to record the happy event. What a momentous occasion. This was to be our first Christmas with our seventeen children.

All we had to do was go upstairs and knock on big Mary Ann and Tish's bedroom door to wake them up and the rest is will be history. I expected the excitement to go through the house like wild fire. But, as they slowly came down the stairs, after about only four hours sleep, in their pajamas and bathrobes, wiping sleep from their eyes, I was recording this with my movie camera.

"Hold it. That won't do," I said as I stopped the camera. "Everyone back! That's no way to enter Santa Claus's room on Christmas morning. Everyone back out and come back in excited. This time, show some feeling, joy and happiness for the movie camera. Look surprised. Now when I count three come back in with some enthusiasm."

Out they all went and I reset the camera to 'on'. "One, two, three come on in now!" I shouted.

They were all good actors. I recorded their "surprised" looks and excitement. The presents were passed around until they found the person with their name on it. After a few hours, they took their treasures up to their rooms and went back to bed to catch up on some much needed sleep.

After Christmas, the whole family hated to take down the Christmas tree. As long as it held its beauty and the needles didn't shed too badly, we would leave it up. That first year, the tree stayed up until February. One year, the neighborhood talk was, that spring was not far away, the Arsenault / McMillans finally threw out their Christmas tree.

Easter

Easter time was another annual family event. We always had an Easter party and the rabbit costume was taken out for the occasion. The Easter Bunny would show up on Easter morning to start the festivities when the family would gather around to start the traditional Easter Hunt. As part of the hunt, children had to find their Easter basket, which had their name on it. There were nineteen baskets hidden all around the house. Many were behind doors and in closets. If you found a basket and it didn't have your name on it, you just left it and continued to look for your own basket. Some baskets were in some very unusual places. And some baskets were nowhere to be found. I suspected that some baskets were changed from place to place so the owner had to keep looking not realizing that it might be where he had already looked. When you found your own basket, then the fun was to continue to look for those who had not found their basket just so you would know ahead of them where it was hidden. Then you would watch them searching for it. As I said, the last one would sometimes be changed to different hiding places two or three times. This alleged conspiracy was said to be among the older children having fun changing the hiding place of the basket just in the nick of time. However, this alleged conspiracy was never proven.

All in all, the holidays provided a time when all the family would enjoy the festivities. Whenever the family congregated, they enjoyed each other's company and there were always enough people to have a party and it's still like that today.

XVIII

Taxes

---

*The worth of a state, in the long run, is the worth of
the individuals composing it.*
John S. Mill 1806-1873

The world is filled with good guys and bad guys and every one of us has a little good and evil somewhere inside. The task is to accentuate the good and eliminate the bad. Seems simple enough. Somebody said, *there's a little bit of bad in the best of us and a little bit of good in the worst of us, so it ill behooves any of us to talk about the rest of us.* This thesis has been around for a long time and holds true in all walks of life and even in governments. Fate has a way of surprising us with the unexpected whenever we find life getting dull. For example, in September, a few years after we were married, I received a letter from the Internal Revenue Service of the United States government, which included this statement.

*In examining your Federal Income Tax return for
The above year, we find that we need additional
Information from your records to determine your
Tax liability. We have arranged an appointment
As we have shown above. Under the law, taxpayers are re-
Required on request to substantiate all expenses and
Deductions.*

"Here we go," I said to Delores. "The IRS doesn't believe we have seventeen children. I just knew this would happen."

"What do you mean, they don't believe us?" Delores said. "You just go down there and tell them they can come to our house and see for themselves."

"Oh, I know. But, you can't just go down there and tell them to come and see for themselves. They want evidence. When the IRS wants to see your records for expenses, they usually want to look at everything. I'll just have to go down there and take all my records with me and also I'm going to take a copy of the front page of the Detroit News article on our marriage as evidence."

"Well, you're an accountant. I'm not worried. I'm sure you have all the evidence that you'll need."

"Easier said than done. In the first place, anyone can make a mistake, even accountants although, I'm pretty sure I didn't make any mistakes. It must be the number of dependents changed from last year that they want to check. And, while they're checking my dependents, they probably think, they might as well check everything."

"Well, just do the best you can dear," Delores said. "Besides, if they put you in jail, think of all the mail you'll get from the children."

"Thanks, Delores. Remember, you signed that tax return too. So, maybe we should go down to the IRS together. That way, if we go to jail, we'll both be getting a lot of letters from the children."

"No sir. That's your job. But don't worry about it, George," Delores said. "Remember, the IRS is made up of people just like you and I trying to make a living…just ordinary people. You go down there and straighten them out and that will be the end of that. I know you can do it."

"I hope so," I said.

Really, I thought, I shouldn't have to worry. I have nothing to hide. If I made a mistake, so be it. I'll just correct it and pay them the difference. Anyone can make a mistake on these complicated income tax returns. I'm only human. They still sell pencils with erasers on them. The only person who can't make a mistake on his income tax is the guy who doesn't submit one and that's a bigger mistake. All I need to do is take all my canceled checks and pay stubs with all my receipts and me and records that I used to fill in my tax return plus my copy of the return. The big photo on the front page of the Detroit News should be all the evidence they need of my new status as a father of seventeen children and a new wife. All the names are in the story so why should I worry. I always thought that they might not believe this anyway. Sooner or later, they were bound to ask questions and it might as well be now and get it over with.

After the forgoing analysis and processing in my mind, I felt better about the IRS inquiry. I was sure that I had covered all the bases and I was ready for my appointment.

The IRS

The day was cloudy when I entered the U.S. Federal Building in downtown Detroit. The reckoning with the IRS had arrived. The receptionist directed me down the hall to room 201.

Mr. IRS Examiner was waiting for me and he greeted me at the door. "Come right in, Mr. Arsenault," he said as I entered. The receptionist must have called him and told him I was coming, I thought. He closed the door behind me.

"Have a seat," he said, and went behind his desk.

Come into my parlor, said the spider to the fly. I thought.

"I see that you brought your records," he said, pointing to my briefcase.

"Yes! I didn't know exactly what you wanted, so I brought everything that I could think of that would help straighten this mess up," I said, opening my briefcase and taking out some of the papers.

"Did you bring all the birth certificates for your seventeen children?"

"Birth certificates?" I said. "Well. No. I'm not even sure we could find birth certificates for all seventeen children. I didn't realize the you would want birth certificates."

"Well, that's your best evidence of the children that you claim as dependents."

"As I said, I don't even know if we have birth certificates for all seventeen children. I know I haven't seen any of the McMillan children's certificates. I'm pretty sure that we have all the baptismal certificates but I'll bet we don't have all the birth certificates. I guess I could get them from the city records for a fee, right?"

"Right!" he said. "The baptismal certificates would help, but I guess that you didn't bring those either, right?"

"Right," I said. "That's where I slipped up. I never thought that you would want them."

"Well, we will need some evidence that the seventeen children are really your dependents."

"Here is the front page of The Detroit News for the day after we were married," I said pulling out the paper and hastily handing him the paper from my briefcase. "That could be used as evidence. Can't it?"

"Hmm," he said, as he carefully began reading the story. Looking up he said, "So you're the guy with seven children that married the widow with ten children from Grosse Pointe."

"Yes, I'm the guy," I said, emphatically as he kept reading.

When he finished reading the whole story, he said, "I remember reading this a couple of years ago. I told my wife, "Here's a couple not afraid to raise a large family in this day and age."

"Well, we're doing our best, and I think we're winning,"

"You both deserve a lot of credit. God bless you. I think that anyone raising that many children shouldn't have to pay any taxes at all."

"Thank you very much." Boy, I thought, I've got the right guy this time.

"I'll take a quick look at the rest of your records, but I'm sure that everything else is all right. Do you mind if I keep this newspaper clipping for our records?"

"By all means. You're welcome to them. I brought them especially for you."

He got up and said, "I'll be right back," as he walk to the door with the newspaper clipping in his hand. When he returned in a few minutes, he said, "I'm giving you a clearance on all your tax returns up to this date. You won't have us bothering you for any of them."

"Thank you very much," I said as I put my records back into my briefcase. Man, did I come to the right place, I thought as I was leaving the building. Now, there's a smart man. First order of business when I get home…get birth certificates for all seventeen children. Note: the IRS never asked about my dependents again.

XIX

The Final Analysis

Nothing is nobler; nothing is more venerable than fidelity.
Faithfulness and truth are the most sacred Excellencies
They are the endowments of the human mind.
Marcus Cicero -106-43 BC

The marriage was a huge success because all nineteen contributed to our magnificent venture. All seventeen children made their own contributions with their best foot forward from the very day we began to plan this union. It was because of each one's total commitment to the family with each doing their part that the venture worked so well. It has been my experience that when more than one agree on a goal, that goal is more attainable by the multiple of those that agree. Thus the *multiple progressions phenomenal* were one of our strong points. It's like the tide in the ocean. *Once the tide starts to come in, there's no way you can hold it back.*

For example, Delores and I were mom and dad. This decision came right from the children in the very beginning of our marriage. The older boys had come to me and asked me what I wanted to be called: George, Mr. Arsenault, father, dad?

I said, "Call me whatever you are comfortable with."

They went out and in a few minutes, they came back and said, "We've decided to call you *dad.*"

And it's been *dad* ever since. That was a vote of confidence for me. I knew they were all smart children. They had realized the value of our objective goals we had set for our union. Once the commitment was made in good faith, we did not waiver from our goal. The rest was easy. "I am as constant as the Northern Star," *Caesar* had said. And, so were we. We were firm on our mission.

"Will God with our petitions in prayer help us to succeed?" That was another question in our minds. If God is almighty, then it follows that He can do anything. Therefore, if we could get God in our corner, we'd be sure to succeed. However, I realize that God makes no *special deals*. You can't say to God, "If you do this for me, I'll do this for you." Sorry, no deal. The answer is as I've said before: Work as if everything depended on you and pray as if everything depended on God.

So, what was the answer? Like Thomas Edison once said, "*genius is just plain hard work.*" The success of our marriage, or any marriage for that matter, is *just plain hard work*. However, I would grant that one must start out with good raw material. We had good raw material, seventeen great children. I told Delores that someday there will be seventeen shining jewels in her crown when she gets to heaven.

Years ago, I read an axiom, "eagles don't see flies." This always stuck with me. Eagles are so majestic that they are not concerned with flies. It meant to me that one should not let little things bother them. It meant that I should aim high and not let little things upset me.

One of Delores' many talents was ceramics and she was aware of my fascination for the flying wing spread eagle. She made me a *wing spread eagle*. Not one that sits on a ledge, but one that was in flight, and I used this as a symbol of our family. My philosophy was to be majestic enough to overlook small mistakes and overlook the small troubles of life and keep your eye on the sky and fly high enough to see the big picture. Another analogy I made involved lighthouses. Lighthouses are beacons in the night for aid to those that are lost and I've tried to be a beacon for our children, hoping to show them the safe way. Delores also made me a ceramic lighthouse for my desk.

If I learned anything in this endeavor of raising seventeen children, it was this:

Children are little individuals…real people…very important people and very special people with all the talent and potential for being good. Delores and I saw us as the children's teachers, coaches, and guides. We did not do our jobs as disciplinarians but rather as teachers. We were not enforcers of statutory laws with punishment. We believed that violence begets violence and love begets love. Therefore, violent discipline as punishment actually teaches the child that it is permissible for big people to hurt small people. This may be the reason that there is so much violence in the world. The wrong lesson is being taught to our youth. When behavior needs correcting, we learned to use other methods and strategies to alter a child's behavior rather then physical punishment. The old adage "spare the rod and spoil the child," in our mind, is wrong. For example, a non-violent consequence could be "go to your room," or "go stand in the corner," depending on age. The word *grounded* was well understood by my teenagers. "You're grounded for a week," was a sentence to be avoided. This was the non-violent discipline preferred.

Behavior modification starts by giving the children a good self-image. "Our children are all good children," was a statement often heard by our friends and neighbors from Delores and me. When children hear this being said to others, they have a reputation to live up to. If they were told that they were bad, then what's to stop them from saying, "I'm bad anyhow, so what!" Not a good image to live up to. The old axiom, *give a man a good reputation and he may try to live up to it*. I believe it was St. Augustine who once said, *you may not be a saint, but if you act like one, maybe you will become one.*

Murray A. Straus, a sociologist from the University of New Hampshire, concluded after his group research on child behavior, that spanking was linked to later anti-social behavior despite social economics, status, or ethnic background, parenting style, emotional warmth and other factors. Thus, corporal punishment, which includes spanking, does not promote good social adults in society. Antisocial behavior like cheating, stealing, lying, being mean to others, breaking things and defiance in the home and in school, trouble getting along with others, may be linked to corporal punishment at an early age. Delores' thesis was that children need to be loved and the earlier the better is true. Like a puppy dog, they will love you back. They see the world through the parent's example. I always agree adamantly with Delores.

It has always been my opinion that what everyone really needs is wise and benevolent counseling. We would have all benefited from this type of learning. While Delores and I may be lacking in wisdom as parents, we asserted that our loving benevolence was boundless. We love them all very much for all the happiness they have given us all these years. The secret of a teacher is that sometimes the teacher also learns many things along with the student. So it was with us.

So if we've gained any wisdom in our journey as parents of seventeen, we wish to leave it for them in this book. As time goes on, every one of us tend to forget all the happenings and events that made us a large happy family. Time and memory make it difficult to remember and convey the lessons we learned on our way to future generations. Therefore, this book is not only a history of events but also all the counseling and problem solutions that Delores and I were able to convey for their edification and practice so that they too can instruct and improve their lives spiritually, morally, and materially and those that follow. But most important, we must *keep the faith*. I've been known to say, "if it was good enough for my father, it good enough for me." And as Patrick Henry so aptly put it in his writings:

> *I have now disposed of all of my property to my family. There is one thing more that I wish I could give them, and that is the Christian religion. If they*

had that and I had not given them one shilling, they would have been rich, and if they had not that, and I had given them the entire world, they would be poor. Patrick Henry—(1736-1799)

Our daughter Aileen Arsenault wrote this following poem in 1991 on our 25th Wedding Anniversary.

THE FAMILY
By
Aileen T. Arsenault

The story begins,
As they most often do;
With a man and a woman,
Starting anew...
She with her ten,
And he with his seven;
Decided to wed,
And create their own heaven.

And who would have known,
On that clear day in June,
How two families could become one,
And not a moment too soon.

The two youngest were age three,
The oldest boy seventeen;
Six girls and eight boys,
Filled the range in between.

Though not always easy;
Or fully understood;

The joining of families,
Brought bounties of good.

Our blessings have been many,
Our sorrows soften by love.
As bonds of our family have deepened,
With help from Mark up above.

And so we come together,
To celebrate this day;
All one, though many,
Each in our own special way.

About the Author

H. G. Arsenault is a retired General Motors Senior Financial Analyst and Financial data base programmer with 36 years service and seven years with a Chrysler subsidiary, VPSI, as a Systems Information Director. He now lives with his wife, Delores, in St. Clair Shores, Michigan.

Printed in the United States
55504LVS00004B/25-126